THE NORMAL KIND OF CRAZY

L.J. VOSS

Published by L.J. Voss

Copyright © 2015 L.J. Voss

Editing by Sara Tharen

Photography by Ashlee Brooke Photography

Model: Megan Van Leeuwen

Pig: Pampered Piglets

Cover Design by Bearhive

To my favorite boys, Thanks for putting up with and loving my crazy.

PROLOGUE

Twenty eight years ago….

- June Nelson -

I noticed her walk in a few minutes ago. She looks about eight months pregnant with eyes brimming with tears. Her wavy blonde hair is down and her skin has a slight pinkish tan. Julie heads to her table to grab her order. After looking in her wallet all she orders is water and a side of fries. That's not nearly enough food for a grown woman let alone one who is pregnant.

I head to the kitchen and tell my cook to make an extra cheeseburger. When her order is up I grab her fries, cheeseburger, and then head to her table. Her head doesn't lift as I set the plates down. In fact she doesn't acknowledge my presence at all, she is dazing off in the distance as she rolls her bottom lip between teeth worriedly. Breaking the silence I

1

interject, "Everything all right, hon?"

Her eyes blink a few times before she lifts her head to me and answers, "Thank you." She sees the cheeseburger and panicked confusion fills her voice, "I didn't, that isn't mine, I only ordered the fries."

"It's on the house," I respond.

"Oh no, I couldn't. I'm fine. The fries are enough, really," she protests.

"I won't take no for an answer. If I have to, I'll stand here until you finish it."

That earns a smile from her as she says, "Thank you, it means more than you know."

Not one to beat around the bush I ask, "So are you passing through? Staying?"

Her eyes fill with tears as she fiddles with the fry in her fingers. "I don't know. I don't know what I'm doing, where I'm going."

I pull out the other chair at her table and sit down next to her. "Well, let's start with where you're from."

"Boston."

"Any family?"

She seems to think about it, "No. No family."

Not wanting to pry too much too soon I drop that line of questioning. "Well, if you want to stay, you can stay with me. I'll give you a job here so you can earn some money before the baby comes and then you can come back after the baby. I'm a widow so it's just me."

She shakes her head in protest, "No. I really can't let you do that. You've already been too nice to me."

"Nonsense. I need some help around here and good help is hard to come by. So really you'll be doing me a favor. There's an apartment upstairs that you can stay in. We'll need to do some fixing up before you move in." I see her start to try to refuse again so I continue, "I'm not going to let you say no. I can and want to help. When the time comes, if you still feel it's necessary, we can work out some sort of rent agreement. You look close to having that baby and you don't want to be living in your car when you do."

She wraps her arms around me as she starts crying, "Thank you. Thank you so much. You must be my guardian angel."

I pat her on the back, "Why don't you hang out here for the rest of the afternoon? I can show you around and you can get a lay of the land. Then we can head to my place and get you settled. I'm June, by the way. June Nelson."

Straightening she says, "I'm Delilah Jones."

I leave her to finish her cheeseburger and go and call Mabel. When she answers I tell her about Delilah and the baby. Mabel being Mabel, she immediately asks what they need and if there is anything she can do. I assure her I will let her know more when I know more. Knowing her she's probably rushing out to get stuff anyway.

The rest of the day goes by pretty fast. I show Delilah around the kitchen and office and then leave her to shadow Julie. Later we sit and eat some dinner together. She opens up a little bit more about herself. She is twenty-three. Her mother is a drunk who has no idea who her father is. She left home at sixteen and worked at a diner along a beach in Boston. When the conversation turns to the father of the baby she gets quiet and doesn't go into much detail. They met during the summer and had a short whirlwind romance. At the end of the summer they both knew that it was a summer thing and nothing more. When she found out she was pregnant she decided there was nothing holding her in Boston and she had always wanted to see New Orleans. She packed up and drove down there. After staying a few months, she realized she didn't want to raise her daughter there. Liking the area, she drove around to the surrounding cities but none of them felt right. She stopped here and didn't have a plan past that. Almost out of money and finding no one wanting to hire a woman eight months pregnant, she had no idea what to do. She decided to stop here and get something to eat and then she met me.

Right now she is following me home. I told her about Mabel, and that we would be meeting her for lunch tomorrow. She'll like Mabel. They're two birds of a feather. They're both reserved and soft-spoken, compassionate and kind. I'm more eccentric and adventurous. It's good that Mabel and I have each other. I help bring her out of her shell and keep her on her toes and she helps keep me in line.

Delilah doesn't have much, only a duffle bag and two boxes in her trunk. I grab her few belongings and make my way to the door. Following me, she stops when she notices my garden. I explain, "They're shrunken heads." At the lifting of her eyebrows, I add, "I like them. Regular gardens can be boring. What's more fun than looking at some flowers and suddenly seeing a shrunken head mixed in? It's also fun to see the neighbors' reactions." She follows me inside and upstairs to the guest bedroom. Setting her boxes down I tell her, "Make yourself at home. Are you up for a tour? I can show you around tomorrow if you want to rest."

"Maybe tomorrow. I'm a little tired. Thank you again. You'll never know what this means to me."

"It means a lot to me, too. Richard and I were never blessed with children. Since he passed it's been a little lonely in this house all by myself. I had Charles for a little while but then he passed away. It'll be nice to have someone around."

I notice her start to open her boxes and see a collection of mismatched vintage teacups. "What are those?"

She blushes a little as she tells me, "I've never had the money for nice things. My shopping consists of what I find at the thrift store. These always catch my eye. Something this beautiful shouldn't be mixed in with junk. They deserve a home. I guess I kind of feel a little like them. People pass them by and never see how beautiful they are. They don't see their worth since they don't come in a complete set. My own mother never saw my worth." She gives me a sad smile as she looks up at me, "Silly, I know."

Not wanting to overstay my welcome I walk out the door and just before I close it I add, "Good-night, Delilah."

Eight years later….

I enter the cold sterile hospital room. Tears are already springing from my eyes. I'm glad Mabel is here with Imogen. I don't want her to see or hear what we are going to be talking about. She's old enough to understand what is happening but young enough to not need to hear the specifics.

Delilah manages to give me a weak smile. I sit on the edge of her bed and take her feeble hand in mine. "Hi, sweetie."

"June, did you get the papers?" she asks as urgently as she can muster.

"The lawyer brought them over this morning. I've signed them and everything is in order," I assure her.

Relief washes over her face. There is a new aura of peacefulness surrounding her. I gently squeeze her hand. "I'll take good care of her, Deli. She won't forget you." I choke on a sob.

In the last eight years, Delilah has become the daughter I never had. Ever since that first night we met we've been there for each other. I was there when she had Imogen and gave her my middle name, Cordelia. When she got sick a few months ago neither of us imagined that it would be cancer and that it would be as aggressive as it was. With a prognosis that wasn't promising and chemotherapy only delaying the inevitable, she made the decision to enjoy that last few months she had. Mabel and I took her and Imogen to the beach and to Disney World. But in the last couple weeks things have taken a turn and we knew that the end of her struggles was coming.

She asked me to take over guardianship of Imogen when she first got sick. I agreed without hesitation. That little girl has become the center of my world. She's smart and funny and gets her sass from me. My heart hurts to think that she won't have her mother here to help raise her.

Guessing where my thoughts are going Delilah says, "She's lucky to have you, June. She'll be so loved. Between you and Mabel, she'll have everything she ever needs. You never hope that someone else will raise your child, but I couldn't have picked better people. With you, Mabel, and Imogen, I found my complete set. Even if I could live a thousand lives I would never be able to tell or show you enough how much you mean to me. I love you."

"I love you too, sweetie. You and that little girl are my world and I can't thank you enough for all you've given me." I give her a gentle hug and we both cry as we hold onto each other. There isn't any way you can prepare to say good-bye to someone you love. I want her suffering to end and for her to be at peace but I'm not prepared for it and it doesn't make it any easier.

A gentle knock at the door followed by Mabel poking her head inside signals she's brought Imogen to come and say good-bye. Imogen follows Mabel into the room with her little head cast down. As soon as she sees her mom she comes running and climbs up the bed. She cuddles her mother's side, buries her head into her shoulder, and then starts to cry. Delilah wraps her arms around her tiny daughter and holds her through her tears. She runs her hand down her hair, comforting her. Pressing small kisses to the top of her head, Delilah looks to be trying to memorize every detail about her daughter.

Not wanting to intrude on their emotional goodbye, I motion to Mabel and we move away towards the door to give them some privacy. Although I'm trying not to eavesdrop, I can still hear bits and pieces of what is being said. I hear when Delilah gives the necklace she had made to Imogen. Before she got sick we would have contests on who could find the most wish puffs. Then we would grab them all together, make our wishes, and blow as hard as we could. Millions of little dandelion seeds would go flying into the air, dancing on the wind in every direction. When we realized how serious the cancer was Delilah had a single seed pressed between two pieces of glass and made into a pendant. She tells Imogen that her only wish was that she could stay here with her but she is too sick and she isn't able to. She explains to Imogen that this necklace is special. Anytime she is missing her, she can rub it and know that wherever her mom is, she is thinking about her and loving her. I chance a glance at them and see Imogen's small head bob up and down in acknowledgement. My eyes shift to Delilah and I see the tears running down her cheek.

I turn away again until I can hear they are done. Imogen climbs off the bed and comes over to us, her little hand clasped around her necklace. Mabel takes her other hand and asks if she wants some ice cream as she leads her out of the room. I can't stop the tears from flowing down my cheeks. Delilah's eyes catch mine and there's nothing and everything left to be said. I wrap her in my arms and whisper into her ear, "It's okay, Deli. You can rest now. It's okay to go. I love you, sweetie."

I hear the monitor signal that her heart has stopped beating. Nurses come in, followed by the doctor and I take one last second before I let her go. No attempts are made to try to bring her back. She was very clear about wanting a do not resuscitate order in place. I wipe the tears from my eyes and look at her one last time as the nurses and doctor call her time of death and start unhooking her from the machines.

The lights in the hall are blinding as I go to find the little girl whose life will never be the same. With each step, I promise to make Delilah proud and to never let Imogen forget her.

CHAPTER ONE

Present Day

-Imogen-

"Gahhhh," I growl as I slam the lid on the espresso machine. I have Rice's number halfway typed in my phone as I make my way to my office. This is the perfect start to my Thursday. I'm shoving papers out of the way when he answers.

"Again, Sweets?"

Just his voice sends shivers down my body and butterflies to my stomach. "Please? You know I open in an hour."

"I'm already on my way with your delivery. I'll be there in a few minutes."

"I beyond owe you! I have a Gouda and ham croissant waiting with your name on it."

Looking around my mess of an office, I set my phone down. That stupid espresso machine will be the death of me. If profits keep going like they have been I should be able to replace it in about a year. I just have to keep it going until then. June would give me the money if she knew I needed it, but there's no way I'm going to let her do that. Thinking of June reminds me of her contest tomorrow. I chuckle as I think how Mabel is going to react when she gets up there. Only June would enter a swimsuit competition meant for women half her age. If she didn't have Mabel to keep her in line, I can only imagine the kinds of trouble she would get into.

She once tried to buy a huge box of condoms when I took her grocery shopping. She said it was because she wanted to see the look on Ol' Bertie and her biddies' faces as she walked back into the retirement home with them. Luckily, Mabel was able to talk her out of it and instead she bought a men's fitness magazine with a half-naked guy on the front.

I unlock the door to the café, head back to the kitchen, then take the Bundt cakes out of the oven and set them on the counter to cool. The Artful Blend is my baby. I was in a pretty bad place emotionally when I left college and came home seven years ago. I didn't know what I wanted to do with my life, I had gained 40 pounds, just been dumped by my boyfriend and was really depressed. June had already sold her house and had moved into the retirement home with Mabel, but let me stay with her for a couple of weeks before she kicked me out and said I needed my own place. Handing me the keys to this building and some startup money, she told me to follow my dreams.

It was The Burger Hut when she and her first husband opened it. She closed it when my mom passed away so she could focus on raising me. She always said she was lucky to marry men who had made sure she was taken care of so she didn't need the money. It kept her young and her mind sharp but with an eight year old to raise she didn't need it anymore. So it sat empty and collecting dust ever since. She has had multiple offers throughout the years but never sold it. The idea of keeping it, just in case, always kept her turning down their offers. I decided on a pastry and coffee shop. Some of my favorite memories of my mom are when we would bake together. Plus she loved coffee so just the smell reminds me of her. She would be proud of me if she could see it. It's always busy here and it combines some of my favorite things: coffee, baked goods, and art.

Remodeling the shop from a diner into my vision took some work. I love to get my hands dirty and loved doing a lot of the work myself. Luckily my best friend Kelly married a very handy contractor who agreed to help expose the old brick walls and wood beams in exchange for free coffee and treats for life. It was a bargain I couldn't say no to, especially since he would get those anyway. It turned out to be exactly as I had imagined it. There are exposed brick walls, wood floors, and a huge chalk board wall behind the counter. It is in the middle of Main Street and a prime location. I would never be able to tell June thank you enough.

Rice walks in as I'm setting the Bundt cake out on the display. He is the walking embodiment of what your mother warned you about, tall, at least 6'4", with a body to die for and at least a few tattoos that I've managed to catch little glimpses of. Top that off with short brown waves I want to run my fingers through and a beard that would tickle in just the right places. My mind drifts back to that day about five months ago when he walked into the shop. He was just starting out his roasting company and wanted to have me try a sample. He said after I did, it would be impossible for me to not want to sell his coffee. I took one sip and he was right. His coffee is amazing and unrivalled. We've been in this tug of war limbo for months, neither one of us making a move, but there is something brewing between us. Today he is wearing a mint green Henley with the top button undone showing his olive skin with a sprinkling of chest hair sticking out and jeans that do glorious things to his…

"My eyes are up here, cupcake," he says through a smirk, "and, by the way you were looking at me, I'll have to insist you buy me dinner first. I'm a lady."

Absolutely mortified that he caught me checking out his package, I manage to stammer, "Don't flatter yourself, Rice, I zoned out while I was running through bills in my head," as my whole face turns a bright shade of red. I'm not one of those lucky girls who can just have her cheeks turn an adorable shade of pink. Nope, my whole face turns red like a tomato. Followed by my ears and my neck and then my chest is splotched with the same red color. He is still smirking at me as he takes my delivery to the back. His coffee is the best in the state which is why his is the only coffee I use here in the shop. People love it so much that I have to have him deliver three times a week instead of the usual once or twice. Not that I'm complaining, seeing him is more of a wake up than two shots of espresso.

I hear him tinkering with the espresso machine when the timer for the cinnamon rolls goes off. I take them out and realize I'm short a display stand. Dragging the step stool over, I climb up to get one off the top shelf.

"It was the tubing again. I fixed it but it's more of a band aid to get you through until I can get a new part here." I turn as I hear him and lose my footing. Great, I'm going down and it doesn't look pretty. You know the blushing thing? Some girls are the same way with falling; they just have a grace that I wasn't blessed with. This is why when Rice moved with lightening quick reflexes to catch me I somehow ended up with his face pressed right between my boobs. I'm fairly confident in my own skin but being pressed up against the body of this perfect Adonis, Gisele would be questioning her figure. If I'm being honest I have a little left to lose but pressed against his hard chiseled body I felt like those ten…ok, fifteen…fine, twenty pounds, were forty. There wasn't a graceful way to get off him and in my fuddled brain sliding down his body seemed like the logical thing to do.

I'm finally face to face with him and looking into his piercing blue eyes. I can see the internal battle raging in their depths. Finally, one side wins and he raises his head as he presses his lips to mine. His tongue tangles with mine as I gasp when his hands press my body further into his. He takes like bubble gum with a hint of coffee. I think that is my new favorite flavor. My hands are grasping his shoulders as if they can anchor me to this moment. After what feels like an eternity but at the same time not nearly long enough, I feel a light tug on my hair his hands are firmly but gently pulling my head away from his.

"Cupcake, we can't do this," he sighs as he lays his head back against the cold cement floor. Rejection, hot and searing, washes over me as I scramble to get off of him.

"Sweets," I hear him yell after me.

The slamming of my office door cuts off whatever else he was going to say. I slide down the door as the embarrassment sets in. How could I do that? Sure he's been flirting with me for the past few months but it's probably his personality and how he is with everyone. I don't even *know* him; I don't know anything about him. Rolling over I crawl and grab my phone. I send a quick text to Michael: *Margaritas my house 8:00.* I'll just tell Kelly when she gets here for her shift. My phone dings instantly with his response: *YAASS.TTYL beezy ;)*

Allowing myself only a few more minutes to compose myself, I open the door a sliver to see if he is still here. Luckily he's left. It just goes to further prove my point that I'm a certifiable idiot. Our kiss obviously didn't mean anything or affect him the way it did me. Maybe I'm the only one feeling this tug of war. Good thing we open in a few minutes. I'll have a whole day of customers to get my mind off of him and the fool I made of myself.

It's been a constant stream of customers by the time Kelly gets here for her shift at ten. She bustles in from the back with a new plate of croissants, her black corkscrew curls bouncing along her shoulders. Kelly and I have been best friends since elementary school. We were in kindergarten together and hit if off on the first day and have been inseparable ever since. Glancing at the clock I notice it's almost *that* time. I grab a cinnamon roll and put it on a plate and get a black coffee, no cream or sugar ready.

He is walking through the door as I turn around. I grab the counter to hold myself up as he makes his way toward me. He is a Greek god. A Greek god in a suit. A Greek god in a perfectly tailored suit with the most stunning hazel eyes I've ever seen. It's been three weeks since he first walked into the shop and the most we've said to each other was, "What can I get you?" "Coffee black, no cream, no sugar and a cinnamon roll." "That'll be seven dollars and seventy-two cents." Then he pays and makes his way to the front table where he sits on his laptop working for a good half the day and then he leaves and it repeats the next day. Although now I don't even ask

19

what he wants, I have it memorized. I once asked him how his day was and he seemed annoyed and confused as to why I was talking to him so I don't try anymore. But that doesn't stop me from drooling over him and dreaming about him at night. Kelly bumps me and hands me a towel as she whispers, "You have a little something," gesturing to the side of her mouth.

I slap her hand out of the way. "It just shouldn't be legal for a man to look like that. He is perfection. Well, almost perfection. His stellar attitude could use an adjustment but I couldn't have dreamed up a man more perfect than him. Oh, which reminds me, margaritas at my house at eight and this one is a doozy."

"Seriously? How can you expect me to wait all day to hear it?" she demands.

"Because, I promise it is worth it and I can't bring myself to talk about it yet. I'm choosing denial and pushing it from my mind for the rest of the day."

"Oh boy, this sounds good. Are you sure we can't close early?" I roll my eyes at her so she continues, "So, anything new happen with Wall Street, over there?"

"No, just the usual. He comes in around 10:15 a.m., I have his coffee and cinnamon roll ready, he sits down and gets to work and that's about it. All I know is his name's Brett and that's only because I had to ask him once when he came in."

"I'm just glad we get to look at him. He can sit in the corner being beautiful as much as he wants. He's the best looking thing in here and if you tell Ben or Michael that, I will kill you and hide your body so no one can find it. Ben would go all cave man on me and Michael would ask about his art hung up on the walls. I'm sorry, but I just don't get it. It looks like he took paint and threw it on a canvas. Although if Michael were here he would agree looking at that fine piece of man is better than art any day. So, is June excited for her competition tomorrow?"

Chuckling I answer her, "Yes, she's picked three swimsuits and one is a bikini. I'm going to have to have the paramedics on standby if she gets up in the bikini. I think Mabel might have a heart attack. I have to give her credit though, she has guts and spunk. Can you imagine if she actually won?"

The rest of the afternoon flies by and I'm dead on my feet as I'm locking up at 7:00 p.m. I head to the back door and climb the stairs up to my apartment. The clicking of little feet on the wood floor and a happy little squeal reminds me I haven't let Mr. Darcy outside at all today. "I'm sorry, sweetie, momma is tired and the gang's coming over. We'll go out tomorrow,

I promise!" I scoop him up on my way to the kitchen and snuggle into his little pig snout. Thank goodness he's litter box trained or there would be a lot of accidents while I'm gone during the day. I make a mental note to clean up my apartment since I can barely maneuver around my room without stepping on clothes. Vintage clothes are my passion and I treat those babies with respect but it usually takes three or four outfits before I decide on one and putting them back on the hangers while I'm trying to get ready seems like too much work.

My apartment isn't huge, a kitchen, living room, two bedrooms, and two bathrooms but it's all mine and is exactly how I want it. Eclectic Bohemian might be a way to describe my design sense but I don't really feel like I fit into any one label. I like what I like and I don't care if you can't mix red with pink or gold with silver. It's homey and comfortable and where I love to unwind and curl up with a good book. Books are my other passion and I have four huge bookshelves in my living room stuffed with books to prove it.

I glance at the picture of my mom on the mantel and my hand automatically goes to my necklace I wear every day. It doesn't get any easier with time. I think the people who say time heals all wounds are full of it. Some wounds never heal. You just learn to live with the pain and not let it cripple you every day. She was a whimsical kind of person, always believing the best in people and finding magic in everyday things. It's been twenty years and if I didn't have June and Mabel, I can't even imagine how differently my life would have turned out. I've never met my father and don't know who he is. I asked June as I got older, thinking my mom might have told her but June said my mom never told her either.

Growing up with June was interesting to say the least. Everything was an adventure and she always believed I could do anything I put my mind to. She always reminded me to make sure to watch out for the little guy but to not get taken advantage of and to not put up with any crap. Life just seems brighter around her. Mabel was always the comforting voice of reason. She kept us alive.

I've just pulled off my bra when I hear a knock on the door. Pulling my shirt on, I go and let in Michael and Kelly who are in the middle of laughing. "All right, girl, I brought the Tequila so let's get mixing so you can get to spilling! Give me all the juicy deets," Michael says as he sashays into the living room. One might think that when I say sashay I am exaggerating but Michael is the proudest gayest man I know. His dark brown hair is in a perfect coif on the top of his head. His porcelain skin looks even creamier against the bright blue of his sweater and tight black pants. His skin is flawless and void of the freckles that sprinkle my nose. He has an impeccable sense of fashion and I thank my lucky stars he walked into the coffee shop a few months ago asking if I would sell his art. His pieces are amazing and always get sold fast but his friendship is something I wouldn't trade for the world.

"Yes, I have been dying to hear this since this morning. I told Ben I wouldn't be home tonight so let's get this party started!" Kelly said as she hands over the margarita mix and plops on the couch next to Michael.

Pulling out the blender from the cabinet I dump everything in and turn it on. I walk back into the living room with the pitcher. Michael pours all of us a drink and we all take a sip. At their cringes I confess, "I might have added a little more tequila than usual, but believe me once you hear this story you will see that it is necessary." I repeat my encounter with Rice this morning.

Michael's jaw is literally hanging open and in true dramatic flair, he uses his hand to close it. "You slithered down him like a snake? And Rice? As in the guy who has been playing sexual chess with you for months? The same guy who is basically everyone's wet dream," Michael squeals. "I can't even. OMG, can you imagine if you two slayed it?" His arms come across his body like he is pulling open imaginary curtains as he says, "Scene change to white dress, flowers, then a baby. Dibbies on wedding planner, no bats."

"I think you missed the part where he ended it and rejected me."

Kelly playing devil's advocate says, "You don't know that's why he stopped. Maybe he was going to say, 'We can't do this right now since you open in a few minutes.' Or 'We can't do this because I have other deliveries.' I think you need to give him the benefit of the doubt and see what he says at the next delivery." Smirking, she waggles her eyebrows and asks, "Was it good though?"

"There aren't even words, Kel. It was hot. Probably one of the hottest kisses I've ever had. It was like our bodies knew each other and just fit together. His beard tickled and was just the right amount of roughness to be amazingly sensual. And then he ended it and I ran away like a little girl!" I muffle through the pillow I'm hiding my face under, "Why couldn't I have said something witty and mature?"

"Because hot guys muddle our brains and make us lose rational thought. And honestly, I've done worse. You just pretend like it didn't faze you and you slay guys in your kitchen all the time," replies Michael. Reaching to pour more margaritas he asks, "So, other than the embarrassing story, what about your other eye candy? Anything happen with Wall Street yet?"

I sigh as I answer, "No, and I don't think anything will. He is perfect and totally obviously not interested. But I can still drool over him every day and I'll be happy about that. Now let's move on from my crappy nonexistent love life. Kelly is happy and in love with Ben, her very own prince charming in a tool belt, but what about you, Michael? Any hot beef cakes you haven't told us about?"

"Ugh, sadly, no. There was a model I was going to paint but he turned out to be a hetty so I didn't see the point in continuing a professional relationship when all I wanted was a very unprofessional relationship," he says giggling. "I do have a fundraiser next week and the main artist is hashtag dreamy and an otter. So obvi I'll be hitting that. You guys should come with me! We can pre-game and get fabulous here." Kelly and I glance at each other. Normally when Michael says he wants to get fabulous and have a night out we end up with crazy makeovers, wearing ridiculous clothes, and it usually ends with him abandoning us to go hook up with someone or he is crying on our laps. He can see our hesitancy because he adds, "No drama, cross my heart hope to die stick a needle in my eye." Then he starts with his whinny voice and pout, "Besides, all I've been doing is binging on Netflix. It's been so long since I've been out I'm basically Jurassic. The only guys I meet are bears and, *hello*, we all know I want an otter. What do you say? Please? Pretty please?" He goes for big puppy dog eyes and sticks out his bottom lip.

Kelly shakes her head, "I really can't. I'm sorry. Ben and I have a birthday party for his dad."

"Fine, yes. Yes, I will go with you," I finally agree. His excited shrieks pierce my ears as he launches himself off the couch and on top of me. After pressing about one hundred kisses to my face he gets off of me and picks up two movies.

"Which one, *Beaches* or *Magic Mike*?" he asks holding up the DVDs. All three of us look at each other and in unison yell, "*Magic Mike*," as we fall in a heap of giggles on the floor.

I pop some popcorn and the three of us snuggle into each other on the couch as Mr. Darcy falls asleep in my lap. Michael passes out on the couch and Kelly heads to the guest room as I carry Mr. Darcy to bed.

"Hey, Immy?" Kelly softly calls out as she leans against the door.

"Yeah?"

She pauses like she is thinking about what she wants to say and then decides against it, "Thanks for tonight, it's been way too long since we had a girls' night. Night. Love ya."

"Love you too. You're the peanut butter to my jelly." I whisper back as I shut my door. I set Mr. Darcy down so he can do his business in the litter box while I brush my teeth. Then I scoop him up and climb into bed. I snuggle down into my grey and purple comforter as I set my alarm for 4:00 a.m. I'll probably regret all those margaritas when I have to get up in the morning but this girls' night was just what I needed. My life is great. I have wonderful friends and family who are loving and supportive. I have my dream job and I'm my own boss. There's just this feeling that won't go away. Like I'm waiting for my life to start or something is missing. Maybe it's time for a vacation. Exotic beaches and green Scottish hills occupy my dreams until they're taken over by piercing blue eyes that turn into the most hypnotic hazel eyes.

CHAPTER TWO

- Imogen -

What is that pounding? Is that beeping? Then it hits me, the pounding is in my head and the beeping is the alarm on my phone. I groan as I reach over and try to hit the snooze button on the touch screen but all I manage to do is knock my phone in between my bed and nightstand.

"Why in the world did I drink that much?" I mumble to myself. My fingers finally wrap around my phone as I remember the reason for the drinking….Rice and that kiss…. I flip back on my bed with my still beeping phone as the embarrassment washes over me again. At least I don't have to face him for another day. Wait, why should I be the only one embarrassed? I know what I've got to do. I've got to do what Michael said and act like nothing happened. That it wasn't one of the single hottest things I have ever experienced in my life. Knowing it and being able to do are two completely different things.

I shower and get dressed. Then I quietly slip out the front door so as not to wake Michael who is still sprawled out on the couch. There are times when the hours of a coffee shop make me rethink my choice of opening a coffee shop and working in said coffee shop. Right about now I'm wondering why I didn't open a lunch only café. This aspirin better help since today is going to be a long day and then I have June's competition tonight.

Luckily I manage to get all the pastries made and open without screaming at anyone or taking a hammer to my head. When we have sleepovers Kel just starts her shift when she's ready instead of waiting until ten and I'm thanking every deity I can think of that I hear her making her way up front.

"Oh my good heavens, don't you dare let me drink that much again, Imogen Cordelia Jones! And I don't care what you say I'm keeping these on," she says as she points to oversized sunglasses, "because I swear I'm looking directly at the sun and there are tiny men with jackhammers in my head. If you so much as even think about telling me to take them off you can just fire me."

I just laugh and hand her a bottle of water and aspirin. "Are you guys coming to June's competition tonight?"

"We were going to, but Ben decided to surprise me with a romantic date into the city so we're going to have to pass. Plus I don't know if I can compete with her in a bikini; he might be disappointed for the rest of his life."

"I get it. If she wasn't so excited I would try to find a way out of it. Where she gets these crazy ideas I'll never know. Are you still okay to close up tonight? They go on stage at seven so I'm hoping to be home by nine."

"Of course, you know I'm always here for you! Make sure you tell June I'm sorry we couldn't make it. Oh and take lots of pictures because I *have got* to see her in her swimsuit up on the stage."

"I will, I promise. And thank you, you are magnificent and brilliant and I don't think I tell you enough how absolutely amazing you are as a friend. You can still close up a little early since we've been posting we were closing early for the last week. Then you guys can get started on your date early."

"Thanks, Imm! And I agree you don't tell me enough how amazing I am."

I bump her with my hip and we both get back to work. The rest of the day passes by uneventfully and before I know it

I'm racing upstairs to hop in the shower before I have to go pick up June and Mabel. I decide to just let my hair air dry and I'm lucky my chestnut hair dries wavy enough that it can pass as decent. I throw on my favorite vintage dress that just so happens to have been my mother's. It's floor length and is red and blue with a tan flower pattern on it. Blowing a kiss to Mr. Darcy I swipe my keys off the counter and bound out the door and down the stairs.

* * * * *

"Immy, I think you missed the exit. How does my hair look? I decided since I'm going to be on stage it needed to be bigger so you guys can see it from the crowd. I added the flower for a beachy feel and put it on the right side so all the fellas know I'm single. This red swimsuit was definitely the right choice. The boys are going to go wild for me."

I chuckle as I see Mabel in the backseat looking out the window. The look on her face saying if she just imagines hard enough she'll wake up and this will all have been a dream. Mabel's been June's best friend as far back as I can remember. Her hair is now a salt and pepper silver grey and wrinkles adorn her tan skin. She was widowed young and had to raise her daughter as a single mom. Her daughter married a doctor and they moved to Minnesota so he could work at the Mayo Clinic there. They don't get down here to visit as often as they probably should so it's been us three, the three Musketeers, since my mom died. Where June is the life of the party and is always coming up with a new crazy adventure, Mabel is conservative and always puts others before herself. They are complete opposites and can fight like cats and dogs but they love each other and I don't think either would have made it through their husbands passing without each other.

I park and we make our way inside the bar that's holding the swimsuit competition. June is directed to the back of the stage to check in. I grab Mabel's hand and make my way to a table in the front. We're enjoying some fries when the DJ gets up to welcome everyone to the Cougar Swimsuit Competition. The crowd is cheering and hooting and then the music starts.

The first few women look really good, they're probably in their 40s or 50s and looking at them is making me rethink the fries I just inhaled. I'm taking a sip of my Diet Coke when June's number gets called and she struts out onto the stage. I nearly choke on my drink as she starts this sultry slow walk to the middle of the stage. She looks gorgeous in her red vintage swimsuit. Her confidence is evident in every step she takes. Her white hair is in a big puff of white curls on top of her head.

The purple Hawaiian flower she added to get the "beachy feel" she was after is tucked in behind her right ear. She must have put on some shimmer lotion because there is a slight sparkle to her alabaster skin.

The crowd erupts as she bends forward and blows a kiss before she turns and shakes what the good Lord gave her. She continues to pop her hips out every couple of steps as she makes her way off the stage. My ears are ringing from all the noise. I'm slowly realizing that I am in fact *not* going to die by Diet Coke asphyxiation. I chance a glance at Mable out of the side of my eye and I nearly burst out laughing. I don't think her jaw could get closer to the floor if she was a snake and could unhinge it.

The next few ladies come out but it's all a blur. The crowd is cheering with half the enthusiasm they had for June. The DJ hops up on stage and calls all the ladies out. When June steps back on stage the hoots and hollers are ear shattering. The third and second place ladies are announced and awarded their crowns. Yes, they have crowns, okay, well, maybe not crowns exactly but they are at the very least tiaras. They are probably from the dollar store but that doesn't lessen the fact that any woman would love to win one. And if she tells you any differently she is lying. As the DJ is getting ready to announce the winner a chant starts up in the crowd, "Eight! Eight! Eight! Eight!" It picks up momentum and is almost deafening as the DJ shouts into the microphone so as to be heard, "Well the crowd has spoken and the judges agree the winner is number eight, June Nelson!"

The look on June's face as they put her crown on and hand her a bouquet of flowers is priceless. I wish my mom was here to see it. I know she's here in spirit and is probably up in heaven rolling on the floor laughing. Even Mabel looks excited and proud of June. And that is saying something considering you couldn't pay her enough to get up there or be caught dead in a swimsuit.

June makes her way to us but not before being stopped by every table on the way. We've already had three drinks sent over to our table for her. Luckily I was able to intervene and had the waiter take them away. Had she seen them she would have said it would have been rude to send them back and I can only imagine the looks I would get taking her back home drunk and in a swimsuit.

"I told you this red one would do the trick," she says beaming.

"Yes, you did. I'm so proud of you. You looked beautiful up there. If I can look half as good as you at eighty-two I'll consider myself very lucky," I say, kissing her cheek.

"Oh Immy, thank you! But sweetie, dressed in this swimsuit the word you are looking for is hot." She starts laughing at her own joke and gives me a hug.

"We should probably get going. I had a late night and an early morning and my bed is singing my name." I link my arms in theirs as we start to make our way to the front. It takes us about thirty minutes to get out the door because June is stopped another five times by people wanting to tell her congratulations. We're on our way home when she says, "We can't go home yet. We haven't even celebrated my win! I think ice cream is in order."

Smiling I agree and swing through McDonald's to get some McFlurries to commemorate her victory. I obviously forgot about the inspiration all those fit forty and fifty-year-olds were and the fact that I already downed an order of fries because along with my McFlurry I get another order of fries. We sit and eat them in the car while they start asking me about my love life.

"So Immy, any love interests?"

"Mabel, you know I don't have time to date. I am at the café at the crack of dawn. I'm there all day and by the time we close I just want to go upstairs and cuddle with Darcy. Besides I'm still young, I have plenty of time. Isn't that what they always say?"

"Oh Imm, you know I only ask because I love you. I'm so proud of all you have accomplished but work isn't everything. I just want you to be happy and I know that if you gave someone the chance they could help make you happy. You've lost a lot and it would be nice to see someone take care of you," she replies as she pats my shoulder.

"I know, Mabel, and I love you too. I am happy. I have a great life with great family and friends. The rest will happen when it does and if it doesn't, I don't need a man to make me happy."

"I just worry about you, that's all," Mabel responds.

"All right, enough of the mushy stuff. We have to get back to the home before Bertie and her gang goes to bed. I can't wait to see the look on her face when I walk in, in my crown with my flowers." She has the biggest smile on her face and I can't do anything but put the car in drive and head back to the retirement home.

I pull up to the front and let them out. "Want me to walk you guys in?"

"No, you get home. You said you had a long day and were tired. Give Mr. Darcy a kiss and tell him it's from his Nan and drive safely. Thanks again for taking me tonight, it was one of the best nights of my life."

"You're welcome. You know I would do anything for either one of you." I give them both a hug and a kiss and climb back in my car. I start thinking about what Mabel said as I drive home. Maybe I should start to date. I mean, it's been a long time since I had a serious relationship. Kelly keeps telling me Ben has some pretty attractive workers. I'll have to remember to tell her tomorrow that I'm ready for her to set me up.

I park my car behind my building and head in the back door. It's 9:45 p.m. but it feels later than that. I'm ready to head right up stairs to pass out on my bed but I should make sure all the doors to the café are locked and the lights are out. Kelly doesn't close up very often and it would be easy for her to forget to do it.

As I open the door to the kitchen I can see the lights on up front. I'm glad I checked. I bet she was so excited to go have a romantic date with her man that she totally spaced turning the lights off. The hangover probably didn't help either, so I guess I am partly to blame. I make my way up front and see a note from her on the counter:

I can't wait to hear all about June's competition tomorrow. I knew you would check to make sure I locked the doors and turned off the lights. Sometimes you can be the biggest control freak! I love you! I'll talk to you tomorrow!

Love, Kelly

P.S. You're the jelly to my peanut butter.

I chuckle to myself that my friend knows me so well. As I turn around to turn off the lights a noise behind me startles me and I whip around. My hand flies up to my chest as I realize Kelly probably forgot to lock the door and this man thought we were open. "I'm so sorry, but we're closed. I was just getting ready to lock the door. We'll be open tomorrow morning at seven." He's a little intimidating in his black on black outfit. His face is all hard lines and angles. It's obvious his nose has been broken on more than one occasion and he looks like he would tower over my five foot six inch frame. Trying to steady the nerves I'm suddenly feeling, I make my way around the counter to help him out the door. That's when I notice he has a gun in his hands and that it's pointed directly at me.

All rational thought leaves my mind. I hear what sounds like a crack and fall backwards. I'm lying there looking up at the ceiling, my eyes focused on an exposed beam. Then I realize that the sound I heard was most likely him shooting me. My body must be in shock because I can't feel any pain. Which probably isn't good, right? Isn't it always the really bad injuries that you can't feel? That probably means I'm dying. At least I can lay here and die without writhing in pain. I hope Kelly will take Mr. Darcy. He really loves her and I know June can't since they don't allow pets at the retirement home. We learned that the hard way after she tried to smuggle a snake in. Maybe Michael will if Kelly can't. I'm glad I got to see June win today. That'll be a good last memory, I'll hold onto that one. A face pops into my line of sight and I scream, "AHHHHHHHHHH!" I was resigned to lay here and die, but I don't want anything else to happen! That's when my survival instincts kick in and I start thrashing.

CHAPTER THREE

- Calder -

Well shit, I probably could have handled this a little better. Her knee just barely misses the family jewels when I finally manage to pin her arms down as I shout her name, "Imogen!" She freezes and blinks a couple times. Finally hearing her name she looks confused as she whispers, "Wall Street?"

Wall Street? Now it's my time to look confused. Not having time for confusion I get back to why I'm here. Looking her in the eye I ask, "If I let go of your arms, do you promise to calm down?" She manages to nod her head so I continue, "I'm agent Calder Murphy with the FBI. We need to get you to a safe house. I will explain everything once we get there. But right now it's not safe to stay here. There's more guys like him on the way. I'm going to reach for my badge, is that all right?" She looks like a deer caught in headlights but she again manages a miniscule nod. I pull out my badge and show her.

Her eyes don't even look at it. Man, I know she wouldn't know if it was fake but at least pretend to look at it. Reasons are piling up on why this is a shit assignment. I didn't become an agent to get stuck on babysitting duty. I just hope that after this I can finally get promoted to the big leagues.

I almost had a heart attack when I drove by for my night watch and saw a guy in the shop with a gun pointed at her. That promotion would have gone up in smoke if she got shot. I stand and try to make my way to the front door and out to my car.

"Oh thank all the gods above!" She says as she runs her hands all over her body after standing up. "I thought for sure I was shot. I did hear a gunshot right? Wait, did you say FBI? What do you mean FBI? Calder? I thought your name was Brett? And why is the FBI watching me?" Good, she was able to shake the shock off.

"We don't have time for twenty questions. There are more where he came from," I motion to the lifeless man on the floor of the bakery. "My job is to keep you safe and I intend do it." I start trying to pull her towards the door.

She glances at him again, "Oh my gosh, you *shot* him! Like you actually, literally, shot him. And killed him! He *is* dead right? There's a lot of blood, too much blood. He has to be dead." The color drains from her face as she says, "Oh I think I'm going to be sick." I try steering her towards the door again but she rips her arm away.

"The least you could do is let me get some clothes. And I most certainly am not leaving Mr. Darcy here." I've been watching her for the last few weeks, and not only is she hot but she's a decent human being. All the shit life's thrown at her hasn't hardened her. None of that matters though, she is nothing more than an assignment. She folds her arms trying to prove her point but all it does is accentuate her breasts. I'm a guy, we notice those things.

"Fine. You have five minutes."

"Excuse me, you don't have to be so rude. It's not like you're the one being kidnapped."

I tighten my hand in a fist to help keep my patience, "I'm not kidnapping you; I'm trying to keep you safe. It's my job."

"So you keep telling me," she mutters on her way up the stairs. She opens the door to chaos. Her shop is clean, modern, and organized; her apartment is crammed. There are bookshelves spewing books and piles of unopened magazines.

Other than clutter it's actually pretty nice. "Hurry, you have thirteen minutes left."

"I'm hurrying, I'm hurrying!" She shouts at me from her guest bedroom. I hear a buzzing sound as she emerges with an empty duffel bag in her hand, "You can get that, maybe it's your boss telling you to just let me go."

I glance at my phone, "Not mine."

I see her look at hers on the side table by the front door and then her eyes lift back to mine and her face is a mix of panic and embarrassment. She flies down the hall and slams her door shut. "Imogen!" I run to her door and try to open it but it's locked. My shoulder hits her door three times before it finally gives way and flies open. My eyes scan her room taking it all in. The image of her lying on a pile of clothes on the floor with a pig in her hands is ridiculous. As I start to come down from the adrenaline rush I see the pig has the culprit of the vibrating noise in its mouth. The *very* large culprit in its mouth. They come that big? That doesn't even remotely look like real life.

"Don't you knock!?" she huffs as she scrambles to get up. She must realize she is still holding the offending device because she turns red from head to toe. Even her ears look like they are on fire. "This isn't mine," she stammers, "Well, ok, yes, technically it *is* mine. But it isn't mine in the way you think it is mine. I don't use it." My silent chuckle makes her mad and she starts to get angry and defensive. "It was a Christmas present from one of my grandmas." When my chuckling doesn't stop she continues, "Argh, she didn't know what they were. They were in a magazine and she thought they were back massagers. That's why it's so big. She wanted to make sure we could get to the middle of our back." She's only making it worse and I bark out a laugh. Done with this conversation she throws it into her closet and brushes past me around her bed. I try to calm my laughter as she turns towards me and adds, "Oh and 'Agent Calder,' this is Mr. Darcy. Let me know when you're ready to grow up."

I smile at the air quotes she uses when she says my name and then it hits me, "A pig? Mr. Darcy is a pig. No. You are not bringing it with us."

"For your information Mr. Darcy is probably smarter than you are and he uses a litter box. If he doesn't go I'm not going. I'm assuming your boss won't be very happy if you leave me here since obviously I'm probably important if the FB-freaking-I wants me. I mean, that is if you *are* FBI."

I run my hands through my hair and then toss them up in a

surrender position. "Fine, you win. You have two minutes." I would be mad if it hadn't been so funny watching her ramble her explanation. I can't help but add, "Oh and I don't think you need to pack that," I point to her closet where she threw the vibrator, "we won't be gone for that long." A pillow hits my face as I smile and turn out of her bedroom. I've got to remember she's an assignment. Do my job and keep her safe and then get out of here. She could definitely be a complication I don't need. I don't do relationships. My life is back in Boston. And my promotion's going to get me to D.C. I've got to keep my head straight for a week and I'll be good.

"I'm ready."

"Let's go."

"You could help me you know?" She says as she motions to her bag and the litter box and kitty litter. Is it still kitty litter if it isn't for a cat? I grab the bag of litter and her bag and check the stairs before heading down. I'm glad I turned the shop lights off on our way up to her apartment.

We make it to my car without any incidents. I pull out and start heading to the safe house. We've been driving for five minutes before she starts.

"Are you really FBI? And if so, then what in the world do you want with me?"

"Yes, I'm FBI. Once we get to the safe house I'll explain everything." I take my phone out, effectively ending her questions, and hit the speed dial for the field office.

"Agent Thomas."

"Sir, it's Murphy. I have Imogen Jones and we're in route to the safe house. There's a mess that needs attention at the café."

"Very good, Murphy. Report back after you arrive."

"Yes, sir." I hang up and glance at her. She is staring straight ahead holding onto that damn pig like he's a life raft. I can't let myself feel bad for her even though I know she's in shock. And it's only going to get worse when I tell her everything. This is a job and I have to keep it that way. I can't do my job unless I push away my emotions.

Luckily the apartment complex is only about forty five minutes away. I pull in and turn the car off. "I'm going to head up first and make sure it's clear. Then I'll come back and get you. Stay here. Lock the doors."

I head towards the building and do a sweep of the perimeter. Inside I do the same thing to the stairs and the apartment. Everything is clear so I go get Imogen. She's in the same position and doesn't look like she's moved an inch. I tap on her window and she jumps as she looks over at me. I unlock the doors and open hers. "It's clear. We can head up." I grab her bag from the back seat and the bag of litter and head towards the building. "We'll take the stairs. Third floor."

We get to the right door and I unlock it and lead her inside. Inside are the typical generic bare minimum furnishings. I head to the second room and put her stuff down and head back out. She's standing by the front door uncertainty on her face. Her head turns towards me and her blue eyes connect with mine, "This is your room. I need to report in."

She nods as she heads into the room and shuts the door. I call the field office again. I'm looking out the window when he answers.

"Agent Thomas."

"Sir, it's Murphy. We've arrived. Everything is secure."

"Good. Back up will be in position in the morning. Will you be okay solo for the night?"

"Yes, sir. I did a sweep everything; is clear."

"All right, Murphy. Report back at oh-six hundred."

"Yes, sir." I hang up and set the phone on the dining table next to me as I continue to look out the window. It's not the most secure location. The street is right below us and there are multiple windows facing it. I shut all the curtains and head into the small kitchenette to see what supplies we have. If I'm going to be up all night I'm going to need coffee. I'm sure she could use some too now that the shock of tonight has set in. All I find is the instant crap. I guess this sludge will get the job done.

She opens her door and comes out. Gone is her dress and now she's in a tank top and a pair of shorts that could pass as underwear. Why couldn't she sleep in those long old lady nightgowns? I definitely didn't plan on her being half-naked while I babysit her. I appreciate the view but I'm really going to be testing my willpower. I mentally shake my head to clear it and remind myself of the promotion I've been waiting my whole career for.

I've these assignments dozens of times. But the people I'm usually in charge of protecting are old sweaty guys or old sweaty guys' wives and families. And none of them had a body like her. I shouldn't even be on this case. If it wasn't such a high profile witness and my boss promising to give me a recommendation I wouldn't have taken it.

"Here," I say as I hand her a cup of coffee, "it isn't the stuff you serve but it works."

"Thank you," she says as she sits on the couch and tucks her legs under her.

"Where's your pig?"

"Mr. Darcy, he does have a name. He's asleep from all the, for lack of a better word, excitement tonight."

I nod as if a pig sleeping in the next room isn't crazy. I take a deep breath as I start, "Imogen, what do you know of your father?"

"My father? I don't have one. Well, I mean, I have one, obviously, but not in the sense that most people do. To me he was more like a sperm donor and I don't know anything about him or who he is. My mom never told me before she died and she didn't tell June. Why?"

"Does the name John Graziano sound familiar to you?"

"Of course it does, I don't live under a rock. He's the mob

boss who runs Boston. You're not telling me he is my father? You are out of your mind if you think my mom would have been with a mob boss. Nope, no way."

"I know it must be a shock, but John Graziano is your father. Your mother was a waitress near The L Street Beach. Your father was with friends before taking over the family business. At the end of the summer your father went home and your mother left for New Orleans. This leads us to you and why you are here. Your father was threatened, which isn't something new for someone in his position, but then they sent him photographs of you. There were notes threatening you and claiming you're his daughter. Turns out they weren't just claims because proof of paternity was sent. We're assuming they went through your garbage or apartment to find your DNA. Your father is a big family man and doesn't take kindly to someone threatening his family, known or as in your case unknown. That was about four and half months ago. He came to us a little over a month ago with evidence against the person doing the blackmailing if we promised to help keep you safe. I'm assuming he was having a hard time getting to the person doing the blackmailing, or he wouldn't have approached us. The person blackmailing him is Manuel Rodriguez. Are you familiar with him?"

She gulps down some coffee as she manages to look up at me, "No and I'm pretty sure I don't want to be."

"He's the main Boston drug lord and actually has some territories outside of Boston. We've been watching you for the last couple weeks and things looked like they were going to work out in our favor. No one had made a move and the trial is coming up in a few days. Then tonight…well, you know the rest. We need to keep you here for the next week or so while the trial is going and then after that and look at witness protection if we need to."

She takes a swig of coffee as she processes what I just said. "Wait a second, you're saying I'm going to be stuck here for a week? Or longer? No. No, that can't happen. What about the café? I can't be gone for a week! Who will cover? I'll lose my customers! That is if I even have any customers left after they hear about someone being murdered there. Oh no, who's going to clean up all the blood? And what about the body?"

"The FBI have people cleaning up and making a cover story in case anyone witnessed anything or heard the gunshots. He was someone trying to break in and rob the store. An off duty unnamed cop witnessed it." I try for a reassuring voice and pat her knee. That's reassuring too, right?

"Well, that's awfully convenient. It still doesn't solve the whole who-is-going-to-cover-me problem. I'll have to call Kelly and ask her to run the café while I'm gone. What I'm going to say to her? I'm assuming telling her my father, who I never knew anything about, is actually, as it turns out, a mob boss. Oh and just wait, Kel, it gets juicier, there is a drug lord threatening him, by threatening me and the FBI have kidnapped me to keep me safe while he testifies against the drug lord is probably out of the question?"

"No, no you can't say that." I say through a smirk.

"Well, she'll never in a million years believe that I took a vacation and I can't say it was an emergency with June because she'd just come help."

"You're going to tell her you have a family emergency."

"The only family I have are here and she's a part of it. I guess I could make up some obscure aunt." She reaches for her phone and I stop her and hold out mine.

"This line is secure. They're probably tracing yours. We actually should have left it at your place. Turn it off for now and I'll get rid of it."

"Things just keep getting better and better don't they? You are not 'getting rid' of my phone, my whole life is in there! All my work contacts, everything. I may not be some tech genius but I'm pretty sure I know they can't track a dead phone. So I pinky promise not to turn it back on. In fact, you can keep it, just *do not* 'get rid of it.' I know what that means. You're lucky Kelly answers her phone even if she doesn't know the number, just in case she wins one of those contests she's always entering." She snatches my phone out my hand, stands up and moves towards the kitchen. I can hear it ringing and then can barely make out a voice I'm assuming is her friend.

"Hey, Kel it's Imm. Sorry to call so late but I need to ask you to cover the café. I have to head out of town for at least a week. My mom's sister, apparently I have an aunt, is in some trouble and I have to go and help sort things out." I don't know what her friend is saying but I can tell by Imogen's expression that she isn't buying. "Yeah. I just found out about her, the police called and I'm the only family she has." Another pause and she puffs out the breath she just took. She glances at me and I see the corner of her lip turn up before she continues, "Fine, Kelly, you're right, I'm lying. My mom doesn't have a sister. I'm going on a sexcation." Another pause. "Yup. Well, that's the thing. I've sort of been on a few dates with Wall Street. And life keeps getting in the way so he's sweeping me away to have his way with me."

54

I choke on the coffee I was just drinking. I have to give it to her, she still has her sense of humor. And there's that name again, Wall Street; I'll have to remember to ask her about it when she gets off. I hear her friend's high pitched screams on the other end as Imogen nods her head.

"Yes, Kelly, I promise I'll tell you everything when I get back. I'm sorry for lying to you it's just that it's recent. And things aren't really serious so I didn't know what to say. I was just wanting to wait to see where things went. And then with Rice and everything, it was just easier to keep it to myself. I don't know if I'll have cell coverage but I'll call you as soon as I get back. Oh, and I have Darcy with me so you don't need to worry about him." Rice? Who is Rice and what kind of name is that? I haven't seen her go out on any dates and I know she doesn't have a boyfriend. She barely has any friends. Her friend says something I can't make out and she answers, "I know but it was his idea; he just *loves* Mr. Darcy and didn't want to leave him out. Will you tell June for me? He's wanting my undivided attention if you know what I mean." Leaning against the kitchen counter she ends the call, "Always. Love you too, Kel."

She pushes off the counter and sets the phone down. Turning towards me I can see the smile on her lips. "So about that, sorry but she knows I don't have any family. She's been dying for me to go out on a date and I knew that if I told her I was with somebody she would shut up and wait to ask questions until I could give her all the juicy details."

"As long as she bought it and you can calm down. I heard you say it before, what's Wall Street mean?"

Her cheeks turn red as she turns to the coffee pot to pour herself some more coffee, "Oh that, well, when you first started coming into the shop we didn't know your name. We took turns guessing what you did on your computer all day and finally we decided that you looked like you could work on Wall Street with your suit and stuff. And maybe you traded stocks or worked the stock market on your computer. That and you have impeccable manners and are super friendly so that seemed like a profession that someone like you would do."

"You gave me a nickname? You noticed me enough to give me a nickname?" I don't even care she basically just called me an ass. I know I can't do anything about it but it's nice to know I'm not the only one enjoying the view. I head towards her and the kitchen.

"Well, I mean, have you looked at yourself? Have you seen the other people who come into the shop? Of course we noticed you, we're females." She finally turns back towards me with the coffee pot in her hand. She raises it, asking if I want more. I nod my head and just as she is about to pour my cup, the pot shatters.

CHAPTER FOUR

- Imogen -

I've barely even registered that the coffee pot I was holding is now just a handle before I'm flat on my back on the kitchen floor. Calder is on top of me pinning me to the floor. His weight is the perfect pressure and he smells remotely of mint and cedar. His hands roam up and down my body a couple times and I hear him let out a breath I didn't know he was holding. Then he is off me with a gun drawn as he leans against the wall and peeks out of the window. It's about this time that Mr. Darcy comes running out of the room squealing. I snatch him up and rub his ear which always calms him down.

I see Calder lower his weapon and pick up his phone. This time he doesn't wait for the person on the other end to speak. "We're compromised. At least one shot fired, suspect fled, no injuries. Requesting a new location," he rushes. His jaw clenches and his hand runs through his hair. "What do you mean you don't have an alternate location? This is top priority!" He pinches the bridge of his nose and then his demeanor changes and I know that the first person he was talking to wasn't his boss but the person he's talking to now is.

"Yes, sir. I'm not sure what you want me to do, sir." He nods his head then continues, "I don't think we can wait a few days. They've already made two moves in one night." Pause. "Yes." Another pause. "I agree. I have a place we can go tonight and lay low for the next few days, until the next location is set up." He glances at me as he nods, "Yes. Yes, sir. I'll report in on the road."

He puts his phone back in his pocket then comes over and grabs the hand that isn't holding Mr. Darcy and helps me up. "We're leaving. Grab your bags. You have two minutes."

"But I heard something about another location not being ready? Where are we supposed to go?" This all feels like a bad action movie starring some fighter turned wanna-be actor. "Why is someone doing this? They have to know I don't know my dad so why would he care what happened to me? I'm not much of a bargaining chip. This all has to be some crazy dream."

"Imogen. We don't have time. My job is to keep you safe

and I plan to do that. I can't do it here so we have to go. I'll explain where we're going once we're on the road. Right now, I need you to go grab your stuff so we can go. I'll carry you and forcibly take you to safety if I have to."

"You wouldn't dare!"

"Like I said, it's my job to keep you safe and I plan to do that. Any means necessary. One minute left."

I weigh my options for another couple of seconds before I see that he is in fact very serious. I scramble and grab my stuff. Luckily I didn't unpack anything when we first got here. I just laid on the bed trying to come to terms with the fact that I was in the custody of the FBI and then changed my clothes. I grab my dress and stuff it in my bag and I'm done in the nick of time.

"If you want us to get to the car fast you might want to help with my stuff," I say pointing to the bag of kitty litter and my bag. Without another word he grabs them off the floor and is at the door. He still has his gun drawn and opens the door slightly while looking right and then left. Then he, not even joking, motions me forward with his fingers like we are on some covert operation and I'm going to understand what his hand signals mean. I come up behind him cradling Mr. Darcy in both arms across my chest and whisper, "If you think I know what your little hand signals mean, you are out of your ever-loving mind."

He looks over his shoulder at me and answers, "I'm going to be in front making sure the coast is clear. You stay behind me and only come when I motion for you."

Getting sick of his condescending tone, I do a mock salute as I whisper back, "Aye, aye captain." The look he gives me goes to prove that he doesn't have a sense of humor and I am thinking it's a shame his looks are wasted on someone who is so uptight. I mean someone's tried to kill me, kidnap, and who knows what else not once but twice in one night. The only reason I'm not a complete emotional wreck is that I'm still hoping I'm going to wake up soon, that and my complete hilariousness.

We make it down the stairs and to the lobby, where he has me wait with the bags, while he goes and makes sure the way to the car is clear. He comes back and grabs the bags and tucks me under his free arm and we run hunched over to the car. I dive in the front seat as he swings my door open. Throwing the bags in the back seat he gets in, he starts the car, and takes off.

He's about to get on I-12 heading east when I feel my

eyelids start to get heavy. I glance at the clock and notice it's three in the morning. I turn my head towards the window. A small fifteen minute nap is all I need.

I jerk awake and it takes me a moment to orient myself. Everything that has happened tonight crashes back to me and I realize the car has stopped and we are in front of a small convenience store. I can see Calder through the windows paying the cashier and heading back towards the car with a couple of bags on his arms.

He opens the back door and sets the bags down then climbs in and starts to buckle his seat belt. "I didn't want to wake you. I figured you needed the sleep and it would be better if people couldn't ID you. I got supplies for the next couple days."

I sit up and look around as he starts to back out. "Where are we? Where are we going?"

"Right now we're in Covington. We are heading to my grandpa's cabin. Technically my cabin since he left to me. It's a good chunk of land along the Tchefuncte River. We'll only be there for a few days while they get the next safe house ready. I haven't been up here since he died, so sorry if it's a mess."

I put my hand on his arm, "I'm sorry for your loss, Calder.

I've never had a grandfather but I know I would be a wreck if June passed away. And don't apologize, as long as there isn't anyone trying to kill me, I'd be fine with a tent in the woods."

He nods his head. I can tell he doesn't want to talk anymore so I lay my head back down and turn it towards the window. Mr. Darcy is still asleep on my lap. I run his ear through my hand as I replay the events of the last twenty four hours. How can this actually be happening to me? I went from a girl who lost her mother when she was young and was then raised by a surrogate grandmother to the daughter of a mob boss?

It seems as though we've been driving forever but a glance at the clock shows it's only been twenty minutes. I'm about to ask how close we are when he pulls off the main road and onto a dirt path, that can definitely not be called a road, and into the woods. It's bouncy and narrow and I'm starting to second guess my decision to trust Calder when things open up and there is a little clearing up ahead.

I can see the dark outline of a house that looks to be about one story tall and quaint. But out here past the city with no lights I can barely make out much past the front of the car. He puts the car in park and turns it off. Turning to me he says, "I'm going in to turn on the power. I'll feel safer if you wait here rather than try to fumble your way through a cabin you haven't been to in the dark. Do you want me to lock the doors?"

"Do you really think you need to lock the doors? If anyone who is after me followed us I doubt they are going to come up and try to open the door, do you?"

He gives me the cutest smile that shows off dimples on the sides of his mouth I hadn't noticed before. Of course I hadn't noticed them before, the man hardly ever smiles. He closes the door and heads up to the cabin. I look around and try to make out the area surrounding the cabin but it's so dark it all just looks like one dark blur. Leaning my head against the window I can see the sky and the millions of bright stars. It's amazing how many stars there are and how bright they shine when you get out of the city. I'm not sure why my past has been on my mind a lot but seeing the beautiful stars reminds me how dull and lifeless I had become when I was with Sean. I lost myself, well the little bit that I had known about myself. When he broke up with me I thought I wasn't good enough and that I would never be good enough to be loved. But I've discovered since then that we are all stronger than we realize. When we let go of the distractions and limitations put on us, we can all shine bright and be beautiful stars.

The cabin lights turn on and then Calder is making his way back to the car. I unbuckle my seatbelt and gather Mr. Darcy into my arms. Calder comes and opens my door and reaches out and takes my elbow to help me out. I raise an eyebrow questioningly at him. Does he honestly think I can't get out of a car by myself? He must be able to see it in the brightness from the interior car light because he responds, "First, you look like you might fall asleep any second, and secondly, the ground is uneven and hard to see. I don't think you want to face plant."

"Oh. Well, no. Thank you," I let him take my elbow and help me up. He lets my elbow go to grab the bags from the back seat.

"Just follow me and try to step where I step." He makes his way around the front of the car and over the lawn. With the lights on I can see more details about the cabin. It's a one story wood cabin the front porch goes the whole length of the house. There are two wooden rocking chairs on the porch that I can just picture an elderly man and woman sitting in while watching their grandchildren playing on the lawn. It makes my heart break for Calder all over again. I'm reminded of his comment about not having been here since his grandfather passed and I'm moved that he would offer to come here just to keep me safe. Maybe there's more to him than just his perfect good looks.

My eyes dart left and right trying to take it all in. We walk into the main area and it's basically one big room with a little alcove for the kitchen. There are couches on the right and the left of the doorway that look like they've been here a few years but they go with the cabin. It makes me wish I had had the opportunity to go fishing and camping when I was younger. My mom had never done those things so she couldn't take me and after she died June was past her camping and fishing years. Moving further in to the cabin I notice there is an old box TV set in front of the couch on the left that looks like it belongs in a museum. Behind the couch on the left is a dining table with four chairs and just past that there is a small kitchen. The kitchen is dated but has a fridge, oven, stove, microwave, and dishwasher. There are open shelves up above and the bottom cabinets are painted green. The kitchen is L-shaped and there is a door to the outside along the outer wall. A fireplace is off to the right and along the outer wall on the right is a bookshelf full of movies, books, and games. Off the kitchen is a hallway that Calder is heading down. I follow him down and to the first door to the right.

"You'll sleep here. That's a bathroom. I have one in my

room so you'll get that one to yourself," he points to the open door just across that hall and down a little bit. "I'll be there," he motions to the door just past the bathroom. Pointing to the door next to mine he continues, "Closet with towels. The next door over goes down to the basement. Nothing's down there except the washer and dryer. Make yourself at home. Shout if you need anything."

"Thanks, Calder. For everything. For saving me, for trying to keep me safe, for bringing me here even when it's hard for you." He looks at me for a few seconds and I get the feeling he wants to say something but he just nods and shuts the door.

Turning around I see that I have a dresser, a closet, and a queen size bed. The bed is a brass frame and is topped with an old homemade star quilt. The floor is wood and there is wood paneling on the walls. I'll unpack my stuff tomorrow and I crawl into bed. I pull the covers up and to my neck and pull Mr. Darcy close into me. He snuggles into my side and I try to make myself fall asleep.

It's pointless. Minutes ago I was dead on my feet but now I can't seem to get my mind to shut off. I think about June and how worried she will be when I don't check in. I hope she'll buy my excuse like Kelly did. Everyone is so desperate for me to find someone I think they'll choose to believe it even if they don't actually buy it. Kelly knows how to run the store so I'm not worried about that but I still hate making her do it. It's my business and I hate forcing other people to do the work that I should be doing. Then there is the fact that I'm the daughter of a mob boss. How is that even possible outside of a movie? Things like this don't happen in real life. Is he going to want a relationship with me? What if he doesn't? What if he does? Do I want one? Do I have any half siblings? It's all so complicated.

Then there are people trying to kill me or kidnap me or all of the above. What I don't get is why they think doing something to me would affect my father. He didn't even know I exist so why use me as blackmail? Don't get me wrong, I'm happy he doesn't want me dead but it just doesn't seem like I would be the best leverage to get him to do what they want. I still have so many questions and I hope I can get answers tomorrow.

I roll over to my other side and Rice pops into my mind. It seems like forever ago we were kissing in my kitchen. What am I going to say the next time I see him? Where do we go from a kiss like that and then his rejection? I can't not order from him. People come to my shop specifically for the Mezzanote Coffee Co coffee. In light of recent events his rejection shouldn't rate high on my list of things to worry about but I can't seem to get him off my mind. I'll just have to try to find a way to be professional. I'll just stick to ordering coffee. There have to be other people who do repairs and maintenance on espresso machines. I finally start to doze off and another face comes to mind and this one has mesmerizing hazel eyes. I think I might not have such bad dreams after all.

CHAPTER FIVE

- Imogen -

There's a cold wet nose pressed against my cheek and snorting in my ear. Stretching my arms up over my head I roll over and stretch out my legs. I look around the room and let out a breath. So it wasn't all a dream. "We're not in Kansas anymore, Mr. Darcy." I swing my legs over the bed and take him in my arms. I take a courage building breath before I slowly open the door and peek my head out. It sounds like Calder is in the kitchen, so I tiptoe across the hall to the bathroom.

As I make it across I softly shut the door and set Mr. Darcy down on the floor. I turn the light on and brave looking in the mirror. Uh, I look exactly how you would expect someone who went through what I went through last night to look. This is not attractive. My hair is coming out of the messy bun I threw it up into last night. It is somehow greasy, frizzy, and ratted all at once. I have mascara smudged under my eyes. My only

70

saving grace is that I managed to lock myself in here before Calder saw me. Except, I'm now realizing that in my stealth rush to get in here before Calder could see me, I forgot my bag. "You stay here," I whisper to Mr. Darcy as I unlock the door and slowly turn the handle. I open the door and walk right into a very firm very warm chest.

"Oh, sorry," Calder rushes, "I was coming to tell you there's coffee in the kitchen. And some eggs in the fridge. There's also some milk and Cheerios if you are more of a cereal person."

I finally muster up the courage to raise my chin and my eyes lock with his. "Thank you, that sounds good. I'm good with anything, I'm easy." My eyes widen at my choice of words. Michael's right, hot guys muddle our brains. That has to be why I turn into a bumbling idiot whenever I talk to Calder. Ignoring my unintended double entendre I continue, "I was just going to take a shower but…I forgot my bag in my room…."

He practically jumps out of the way, "Oh, I'll just be in the living room. I have some work to do so," he trails off as he turns and heads for the front of the cabin. I quickly grab my bag from my room and rush back to the bathroom. My shower might have broken speed records. I'm anxious to do some more scoping and get to know the place I'll be staying for the next couple of days. I throw my hair up in another messy bun, rub on some moisturizer, and put on old overall shorts and a loose white t-shirt and head out to the kitchen.

Calder is on his laptop at the table. He looks up and I'm rewarded with a little half smile that showcases one of his adorable dimples. I don't miss the sweep his eyes make down my body and I smile back and head into the kitchen. Grabbing the milk and eggs from the fridge I set them on the counter and step back trying to think where a frying pan might be.

"The cabinet on the bottom left of the stove."

I turn towards him and give him another smile, "Thanks. Did you already eat? Did you want some eggs?"

"I ate earlier."

I give him a small nod and reach for the cabinet he indicated housed the frying pan. I start to heat the eggs and milk, mixed together for scrambled eggs, in the frying pan. I grab a mug and poor some coffee. Normally I'm not much of a coffee drinker. I know, who owns a coffee shop but doesn't drink coffee? Chai tea lattes are more my speed. But with the day I had yesterday and the fact it doesn't look like things are going to go back to normal any time soon I figure I could use the caffeine any way I can take it. The coffee makes me think of Rice again. It's a delivery day and that means I would have had to face him. I'm slightly relieved and glad that someone is trying to kill me so I have more time to try to compose myself before I have to deal with my feelings. I guess you can always find a silver lining to any situation.

Once my eggs are done, I go through a couple of cabinets before I find the one with the plates. I pick one and dump my eggs onto it. Heading to the table with my plate of eggs and coffee, I remember that I haven't fed or given Mr. Darcy any water. I set my plate and coffee down on the table and then head to my room to grab his dishes and food. He's already nudging me out of the way to get to his food while I set his water down.

Sitting at the table I dig into my eggs and chance a couple of glances at Calder out of the side of my eye. There's a little bit of scruff along his jaw from not shaving for a day. I have to stop myself from taking my hand and rubbing it along his cheek. The roughness would create an intense pleasure pain sensation during a kiss. What am I doing? I shouldn't be thinking about kissing him! He is only here with me because it's his job. Literally, he is being paid to be with me. That brings to mind prostitutes and I giggle at the thought of Calder working the streets. Someone may be paying him to keep me safe and babysit me but it doesn't mean I can't enjoy the scenery. I just have to remind myself that there is a strict no touching policy.

"So, what's the plan? I know you said we would stay here for a couple days until another safe house is ready but how long will I have to stay with you guys? I have a business I have to run and want to get back to."

"We'll stay here as planned. Then go to the next safe house until the trial is over. It shouldn't be more than a few more days. So if everything goes according to plan, maybe a week. While we're here, make yourself at home. There're books, movies, and games in the living room. You can go outside but I'd prefer if you stay by the house. We're pretty secluded up here but I would rather be on the safe side. I have some work I need to get done and some phone calls to make. I'll be in my room if you need anything." He folds his laptop and stands up.

I'm feeling a little abandoned as he heads back to his room. I wasn't expecting him to entertain me the entire time but I also didn't plan on him locking himself away in a separate room. Every time I think I start to get a handle on him he does something that throws me off. I wash my dishes and set them on the drying rack then turn around to decide what to explore first. My eyes catch the books and I decide to start there. I'm a sucker for a good book.

Looking through the titles, there a little bit of everything. John Grisham is right next to the Hardy Boys, then it's *Jane Eyre* and snuck in the middle is Diana Gabaldon and Susan Elizabeth Phillips. So, someone liked to read and that reading included romance novels. I smile assuming it was his grandma and I think of what a fun person she must have been. You can't love to read and discover new worlds through books and be boring. Each book you read leaves little bit of itself in your soul. And judging by the variety, she must have been very interesting. I grab *Jane Eyre* and make my way over to look at the games. They've got quite the selection, some I haven't seen or played in years. June is a board game fiend, so we always played them growing up. They have Scattegories, which is my favorite. Taboo is another one of my favorites but you need more than two players. Not that it matters since Calder has locked himself away in his room. He doesn't really come across as the board game playing type either.

I look through the movies and it is like I'm thrown back in time. All of my childhood favorites are here not to mention I don't think I've seen a VHS in who knows how long. I spot *Short Circuit* and I'm sold. It's been years since I've seen that one. It was my favorite and I would watch it with my mom at least once a week when I was little. I set it on the TV for later.

Jane Eyre is calling my name, so I plop on the couch and Mr. Darcy curls up in my lap and I dive in. I've always loved this book. There have been numerous movies made based on the book and while they've all been good and I probably couldn't pick a favorite if I had to. None of them come close to the book, although that's usually always the case with movies based on books.

My stomach rumbles when the gipsy woman wants to tell all the young single women their fortunes. The clock on the VCR reads one o'clock, not that I know if it's right or not. I mark my spot in the book and set it down. Darcy darts into my room to go to the bathroom as I make my way to Calder's door. I knock and wait for him to answer.

He pulls the door open and looks at me, "Yeah?"

"I was just going to fix something for lunch and I realized you probably hadn't eaten so I thought I would see if you wanted something."

"What time is it?" He glances at his watch, "One o'clock already? Um, sure. That would be great. Thanks. There's stuff for sandwiches. Your file didn't mention any food allergies. So I figured PB&J would be fine."

My file? I'm once again reminded of who he is and why he's here with me. "No, no food allergies. Peanut butter and jelly is great. I'll just go make us some. Did you want me to bring it to you here?"

After a second of deliberating he answers, "No. I'm almost done. And I could use a break. I'll be out in a minute."

The door closes as I make my way back to the kitchen. Mr. Darcy follows me and I'm just getting done with the sandwiches when Calder comes in. "Here, this is yours. I wasn't sure if you would want one or two so I just made one. But I can make you another one if you want. I was thinking about eating mine out front on the deck if you want to join me."

"One's fine."

Not sure if he intends to follow me I grab the book and head out front and sit in a rocking chair. I hear him behind me followed closely by Darcy. The property the cabin is on is beautiful. It's secluded and quiet. You can really appreciate the beauty of nature while out here. We eat in silence broken only by the creak of the rocking chairs.

"I remember loving it here when I was little. Some of my best memories are at this cabin," Calder says, breaking the silence.

Trying to hide my shock at his initiation of a conversation, I respond, "It's beautiful. You're lucky you had somewhere like this to come to and people who wanted to take you. I can just imagine all the fun memories you must have made."

He looks over at me with a look that is close to sympathy, "It must have been hard growing up without a family and losing your mom so young."

"It was hard losing her; it still is. But I like hearing other people's stories about growing up. And I do have a family. I have plenty of family. My family just includes a lot of people who choose to be included in that term rather than just born into it. I guess my family just grew too. It's crazy finally knowing who my dad is. I thought it would be a bigger revelation." He laughs and I smile at him, "I know you think I'm crazy. Having someone try to kill me twice in one day does seem pretty *big* but I thought it would mean more, emotionally. Maybe it has to do with not having met him and how this all still seems so surreal. He's always been this huge question mark in my life and in a lot of ways, even though I know his name, he still is. I wonder what he and my mom were like together. I wonder what he's like now."

"I imagine it's a lot to process."

"To say the least. Tell me more about your childhood here."

"It was my grandpa's cabin, my dad's dad. We used to come all the time. I learned how to fish here. My grandpa was into the outdoors and loved teaching us. I was the only one who really cared. My grandma loved being with the family. My parents moved to Chicago when I was in junior high and then we only came once a year if we were lucky. I can't believe my grandpa left it to me. I was always his favorite, my siblings didn't care for the outdoors and fishing as much as me."

"How many siblings do you have?"

"Three. My sister is the oldest, then my brother, then me, and then my little brother."

"It must have been fun growing up with such a big family." Each word he spoke about his family was filled with love. He still misses his grandparents. It's evident in the happy sadness in his eyes when he talks about them.

"Usually. Sometimes I wish they were a little less loving and supportive." He glances away and whatever caused him to open up to me is gone. He turns back to me and he's back to his emotionless mask. "I have more work to do. I should get back in."

"I think I'm going to sit out here and read some more. Thanks for eating lunch with me. I had a good time and I almost forgot that there is a price on my head," I say, smiling at him.

"You found my grandma's book collection. She would sit out here reading while we were fishing and playing in the river." Just like that his mask slipped again. It must be the memories and emotions of being up here. "I don't know how you do it. Joke about what has and is happening. You do realize that this is serious and that your life is actually in danger."

"It's who I am. It wouldn't change anything to be cowering in my room scared to death; I'm not going to let the bad guys win. Besides I have my very own James Bond protecting me. Do I really have anything to be scared about?"

He smiles and shakes his head as he heads inside. So there is a softer side to Mister all-business-it's-my-job-to-keep-you-safe.

I pick up the book and resume reading about Jane and the goings on at Thornfield Hall while Mr. Darcy sleeps by my feet. My eyes start to close after I get a few more chapters read. When I wake up it looks like it's almost sunset and Mr. Darcy isn't by my feet anymore. I bolt up and start frantically looking around. Turning towards the door, through the screen I can see Calder on the couch with Mr. Darcy curled up next to him sleeping.

The door creaks as I open it and both Calder and Mr. Darcy look towards me. "You almost gave me a heart attack! I woke up and I couldn't find Darcy and I thought he had wandered off and was alligator food!"

"Alligator food? When you jump to conclusions you really go for it, don't you? I came to get a drink and you were asleep. He was waiting to come inside so I let him in. We got to know each other and we like each other now. Or at least we've come to an understanding," he says with a proud grin on his face as he looks at Mr. Darcy.

"Oh is that so? Well, I'm not sure how anyone could not like Mr. Darcy and as for you I guess it just takes a little bit to get to your gooey center."

"Something like that. There wasn't much at the store we stopped at so for dinner our options are cereal, sandwiches, or reheating breakfast burritos. I'm heading into town tomorrow for more supplies. If you want anything, make a list and I'll grab it while I'm there. I'm going to go ahead and stop that look in your eye: no, you can't come. It's too dangerous. I'll be gone for an hour or two tops. Normally there would be back-up here to keep an eye on you. But since we're trying to keep a low profile we don't want or need the added attention multiple cars driving here would cause."

I let out a huff of air as I answer, "Fine. Cereal is fine with me for dinner. And you better believe I'm making you a list!"

His only answer is a chuckle as he starts taking out the bowls, milk, and cereal. After he's done pouring his cereal and milk he moves so I can get mine and sits on the couch. I fill my bowl almost to the brim and make my way over to the opposite end of the couch. We eat our cereal in a surprising comfortable silence until his eyes land on the movie on top of the TV.

"I haven't seen that movie in forever. It was one of my favorites growing up."

"Seriously? It was one of my favorites too. My mom and I used to watch it at least once a week when I was younger. Most people haven't heard of it when I bring it up. June told me I would wake up in the middle of the night and my mom would put it on so I would stop bugging her and she could get some more sleep. I saw it in the movies and thought it would be fun to watch it tonight."

"I'm done with work if you want company?"

"Of course! I only wish we had some popcorn. A movie isn't complete without popcorn."

"Hold on," he stands and grabs for my empty bowl. I hand it to him and he heads into the kitchen and sets the bowls in the sink. He's opening and closing different cabinets. "There might be some Jiffy Pop popcorn around here. I'm not sure how old it is. But I don't think it goes bad. Here it is."

"I'm willing to try it. Besides you'll eat it first and if you don't die then I'll have some, because it's your job to keep me safe," I say with a smile and a bat of my eyelashes.

He barks out a laugh as he turns to start popping the popcorn on the stove. I get the movie all ready to go and snatch Mr. Darcy up into my lap. Soon the sound of kernels popping is followed by the heavenly buttery aroma of popcorn. Calder plops down on the couch with a big bowl full of popcorn. "Well, here goes nothing. It has been a pleasure to serve you, m'lady."

I can't help but giggle at his impromptu attempt at humor. "Well? What's the verdict?"

"Not bad. Not bad at all. Maybe a little stale but I think it'll do," he extends the bowl out to me to grab some. I take a handful and put a piece in my mouth. Definitely not fresh popcorn, but not half bad either. The movie starts and we sit and enjoy our popcorn in companionable silence. We both laugh at the same places. My eyes start to feel heavy about three quarters of the way into the movie. I know I should get up and go to bed but I'm enjoying this. I haven't been on a date in months. While I know this is in no way a date, it's still nice to have a fun night with someone of the male variety. Michael doesn't count, since he's basically one of the girls.

"You're falling asleep. We can stop the movie and you can go to bed."

"I'm not falling asleep. I know exactly where we are in the movie and everything that has happened. Be quiet so I can hear."

"All right, if you say so."

I nod my head proud of the fact that I won an argument while barely being able to keep my eyelids open. They keep getting heavier and my "blinks" get longer. My last thought is how my life is like the movie. Johnny Five is afraid he is going to be disassembled and there are people after me to do essentially the same thing. How ironic that I picked this movie when it relates to my current situation. Life's funny like that I guess.

CHAPTER SIX

- Calder -

I can't remember the last time I had this much fun with a woman outside the bedroom. She makes things easy and comfortable. It's like we've known each other for a long time and there is no need for pretenses or games. I don't even think she knows how beautiful she is. I look over at her asleep on the couch. She's not one of those girls who are only hot after caking on layers of makeup. She actually looks better without any on.

This isn't good. She's the type of girl who gets in your head and messes things up. I have a plan and that plan doesn't include her, or her pig. Somehow that little runt has gotten in my head too. I'm not an animal person. Probably because it would mean having something relying on me and that could throw a wrench in my plans.

I've got to stick to the assignment. Keep her safe and then get the hell out of dodge. Maybe it's good I'm getting away from her tomorrow. I can get my head back on straight. I throw a blanket I snag from the coat closet on her and head to my room. Getting her out of my head is going to be easier said than done. The last thing on my mind before drifting off to sleep is her teasing smile.

The sun's hitting my eyes through the curtain and the smell of scrambled eggs and toast drifts into my room. I throw a t-shirt and sweats on and head to the kitchen. Imogen is standing in the kitchen dishing eggs onto two plates and there's a plate of toast on the table.

"Good morning," she says with a smile. "Why didn't you wake me up last night?"

"Morning. I figured you were tired from the day before and trying to catch up on sleep. I thought it would be better to just let you keep sleeping."

"Thanks for giving me a blanket. I woke up early and decided to make some eggs and toast and made some extra in case you wanted any."

"It smells good. I'd kill for one of your cinnamon rolls right about now."

"I made a list of stuff for you to get while you're in town. Our dining selection will be better than toast and cereal after that." She sits down and sets a plate across from her for me. I follow her lead and sit down. I take a forkful of eggs and stuff them in my mouth. I savor the flavors as I chew. Who knew scrambled eggs could taste so good?

"These are amazing. Not too runny and not to dry. Do you do something special?"

"Thanks, I'm glad you like them. Actually yes, I add butter to them. I saw Gordon Ramsey do it on a cooking show once and I've done it like that ever since."

I take a few more bites of eggs and grab a piece of toast and spread some jam on it. I notice she's eaten all but a few bites of her eggs. Almost like she read my mind, she reaches down and sets her plate on the ground. "Mr. Darcy loves eggs," she says with a shrug. She says it like it isn't weird to be sharing your breakfast with your pet pig. I'll admit he's grown on me. But it still is taking some getting used to.

She starts to clean up and I go to my room to get ready to head out. When I get back to the kitchen Imogen is nowhere to be found but she's set her list on the table. Her list is more like a novel, I smile as I read through it. Popcorn is listed on there at least three times. I grab my keys and make sure I have my wallet as I head out the front door.

"Don't forget my popcorn." I turn towards her voice. She's sitting in the rocking chair with one leg up and her hands resting on her knee. "I'm serious. Men never ask for directions and always forget to look at the list. I wrote it down four times so you couldn't miss it."

"I saw that," I reply with a grin. "I promise I won't forget. I'll be back in a couple hours. Don't wander off. Don't get shot. I really don't want to lose my job."

"I promise I'll be good and follow the rules. Oh and make sure it's Pop Secret and not any of the others; they're garbage."

"Pop Secret it is," I give her a slight nod and head down the steps and to the car. I'll be lucky if she follows my rules. My plan is to get what I need to done and get back. In all honesty it's not just her safety that is making me hurry. She's not like the women I'm used to dating. She's comfortable in her own skin and she's funny. She gives as good as she gets.

I'm almost into town when I have enough bars to report back in. It rings four times before someone answers. "Agent Murphy reporting in to Agent Thomas."

"Yes, Agent Murphy, please hold." Finally, I hear someone pick up the phone again. I can hear voices in the background but I can't make out what they are saying.

"Agent Murphy, is everything under control with Miss Jones? Is the location secure?"

"Yes, sir. The location is secure and Miss Jones is safe." I drive towards the center of town. "Sir, what's our time line? How long will we be at this location?"

"I don't have an exact answer for you on that. We're still preparing another location. The trial starts tomorrow and we're video-taping Graziano's testimony. I'm going to need you to come in, we have some stuff you need to look over."

"I'm not sure that's a good idea, sir. I think we need to lie low for another day. They're bound to be searching the surrounding areas for any sightings of her. Bringing her in with me is out of the question in case someone spots her. And I wouldn't feel safe leaving her alone here all day." I pull in front of the first grocery store I see and park the car. As much as I'm trying to talk him into us staying here, I'm trying to convince myself that the reason I'm even asking is for her safety and not because I want to spend another day alone with her.

"Fine. Spend another day there. Then I need you in here, Murphy."

"Yes, sir. I have spotty coverage at the cabin. So I'll probably be dark for the next forty-eight hours."

"Very good, Murphy."

I hang up the phone and breathe a sigh of relief. Relief at what exactly? I'm not sure and there is no way in hell I'm going to look into it. Swiping the keys from the ignition, I climb out of the car. I've always hated these town cars. They are too low to the ground. Being six-foot-two, there are challenges getting into a low car. I lock the doors and head into the grocery store.

I make sure to grab some more milk and eggs. Glancing at her list, I see that it's mostly basics - flour, sugar, butter, etc. I chuckle when I see popcorn on the list again. The snack aisle is just a few over so I head over there and grab another couple of boxes of cereal on my way.

I'm standing in front of rows and rows of popcorn. How many brands of popcorn are there? Then I remember she wanted a specific brand. I should have written it down. How can I forget the stupid brand she wanted? I'm an FBI agent. I remember pages of information but a brand name of popcorn is gone just like that. I'll have to buy one of each brand. I don't even want to know what would happen if I didn't get the right one. As I start to grab different boxes I notice not only are there different brands but each brand has different flavors. How am I supposed to know if she wants Butter Lovers, Movie Theater Butter, Butter Xtreme, or one of the other twelve different kinds? Maybe she likes caramel corn. Maybe she's more of a kettle corn person. I know women are all about fat free stuff so maybe she wants the 99% fat free one. Scratch that, she'll probably assume I'm calling her fat and get mad. The only solution is to get one of everything. I chuck the boxes in the cart and head to grab the last few items on the list. A few more things catch my eye as I walk through the aisles so I toss them in and head to the check out.

Looking at all the groceries laid out you would think we were feeding a family of eight. The teenage cashier rings up the first two boxes of popcorn and seeing the rest of the boxes, glances up at me. I shrug my shoulders in answer to his unspoken question and he gives me a nod of understanding. He finishes ringing me up and I grab the bags and head to the car.

I toss them in the back seat and pull out of the parking lot. I flip through a couple of radio stations but the only thing on is some girly pop crap. I turn it off and decide to drive the rest of the way back to the cabin in silence. The silence gives me too much room in my head so I flip the radio back on and settle for the least annoying station. To my surprise, I come across a station playing Steve Miller Band's "The Joker." It's an immediate flash back to when I was younger and driving around with my grandpa. I listen to this station almost the whole way back until the reception gets too bad. Then I drive the rest of the way in silence.

I pull up to the cabin and glance at the clock; it's almost three in the afternoon. The front door of the cabin is open and I can see Mr. Darcy standing in the doorway. When I open the car door I hear music coming from the cabin. As soon as he hears the door open, he starts to come down the stairs to greet me. I realize what she's listening to as I get closer. She continues to surprise me. Who would have thought she would know who Paul Simon was? I give Mr. Darcy's head a rub and then climb up the stairs.

She's cleaned the cabin while I've been gone. Not only that, but it looks like she's organized it. I don't think it's looked this good in years. "Wow, you've been busy. You got all this done while I was gone? The place looks great."

"You aren't mad then? I was afraid you would be upset that

I moved things around. But I was bored and wanted to try to be helpful."

Looking around I notice some fresh flowers in a jar on the table. "I'm not mad at all. I'm glad you found something to do." I turn towards her, "Paul Simon, huh?" I notice she has the same flowers on her head. They're the flowers that grow out in the back on your way down to the river.

"Yeah. I hope it was okay that I went through the cassette tapes. It was too quiet here without you and my imagination started to get the better of me. I didn't even know anyone still had these."

"I told you to make yourself at home and I meant it. I want you to feel comfortable while you're here. You're under FBI protection; it's not a jail sentence. I'd forgotten about those tapes actually. My grandpa loved music. My grandma liked music too but her tastes ran more towards country," I say as I head back out to grab the bags of groceries. She follows me to the car and grabs half of the bags and takes them into the kitchen. I follow behind her with the rest of the bags and set them down next to hers. She starts to unpack the groceries and stops short when she pulls out two different boxes of popcorn. She looks into a couple different bags and then turns

94

to me and raises an eye brow.

I raise my hands in surrender. "I forgot which brand you said. So I was going to get one of each brand. But there were so many flavors and you didn't say which one you wanted. The only solution was to buy one of each. You better really like popcorn, because we're going to be eating a lot of it."

"Oh, don't you worry, I could eat popcorn with every meal. But you really didn't need to do that, Calder. I would have eaten whatever one you brought back. I'm not that high maintenance. I do know what we can do tonight while we eat some of the popcorn you bought." She goes over to where the games are and pulls out Battleship. "I haven't played this game in ages. June used to play this with me every Sunday night."

I continue to unpack the groceries as I answer, "Sure. Just be prepared. I clean up in that game."

She lets out a chuckle, "We'll see about that." So she likes to trash talk. Got to say it's kind of a turn on. We finish unpacking and putting away the groceries. I turn around and notice two fishing poles leaning by the front door.

"Where did those come from?"

She follows my eyes. Her hands knit together as she rushes,

"I went out for a little walk and found some wildflowers I wanted to pick. I wanted to make these flower crowns. I used to make them with my mom before she got sick and totally forgot about them. So I picked some and was heading back inside when I noticed the shed. When I looked in I saw those fishing poles. I've never been before and I thought maybe, if you had time, you could show me how?"

I spin to face her, my shock showing on my face, "You've never been fishing? Ever? Not even when you were younger?" As I finish my last sentence I realize why she wouldn't have gone fishing. She didn't know who her dad was until a few days ago and there haven't been any other male figures in her life.

"No, there was never anyone to take me."

"We're here for one more day, so we can go tomorrow. I'll teach you everything I know."

Her whole face lights up as she smiles and I like that something I said caused her to smile like that. "Thank you! You don't know how much that means, Calder."

"It really isn't a big deal. Plus if we catch anything, fresh fish for dinner beats sandwiches."

"Well, it means a lot to me. That you'd take the time to

teach me is really nice. It's your job to make sure I don't die but it isn't your job to entertain me. It's something I've always wanted to learn. I'm going to go read on the porch for a little bit. But I was thinking spaghetti for dinner, maybe in a couple of hours?"

"Spaghetti sounds perfect." She heads outside and I head back into my room to finish some work I have left to get done. Although that's easier said than done. My mind keeps drifting to her in that flimsy white dress with those flowers in her hair. I've got to stay focused. This, her, isn't the plan. That promotion is my dream. It's what I've been working towards my whole life. It's a family legacy to go into law enforcement. My dad and grandpa both were detectives. I always knew I wanted to follow in their footsteps but I wanted more than just the local police department.

Marriage and kids are nice for some people. They were never a part of my plans. My parents have been married for thirty-three years. They have been the perfect example that when it's right, it works. They fight like cats and dogs. But they always make up and they always choose each other. My only choice was the FBI. I didn't want or need any distractions to take away from that. I still don't.

I thought I could have it all once. But Michelle made me realize my work hours and dedication to the job wasn't fair to anyone in a relationship with me. I don't work a typical nine to five and once I get promoted the hours could be even worse. She worried every time I went to work. It wasn't something she could live with. Especially since she wanted kids and didn't want to worry about their father not coming home. After she left, I've been dedicated to getting that promotion. If I had to decide between a family and my career then the choice was an easy one. My relationships since then have been made up of one night stands.

I spend some time looking through some files and sending some follow up emails. I shut my laptop and head out to the kitchen. Imogen is in there getting stuff ready for dinner. "Is there anything I can do to help?" I ask her.

"No, thanks though. I just need to cook the noodles and heat up the sauce. My mom is probably rolling over in her grave right now. She'd kill me herself if she knew I was using premade pasta sauce. But I didn't want to make it from scratch up here at the cabin. I took the lazy way out."

"It's more than I would have done. If we were close enough I would have just gotten take out."

"It'll be ready in about twenty minutes."

"Okay. If you are sure you don't need my help I'm going to go out to the shed and see what our bait options are for fishing tomorrow."

"Nope, I've got it covered. And, Calder, thanks again for everything. You've made a horrible scary situation actually manageable."

I give her a slight nod and head out to the shed. There are cobwebs all over. I'm surprised she even ventured in here. Most women I know wouldn't touch a spider with a ten foot pole let alone walk into an old shed with cobwebs covering every corner. Spotting my grandpa's blue tackle box I grab it and set it down and open it. Looking inside I see some old PowerBait, dried up marshmallows, and some old red fish eggs. It's probably all too old and dried to use. I'll need to head to the gas station down the road and see what bait they have. I close the tackle box and head back inside.

"So all the bait's too old to use. If we want to have a chance at catching anything we'll need something not dried out. There's a gas station down the road. I'm going to see what bait they have. I'll be back in probably twenty minutes."

"Oh no, Calder, we don't have to go fishing. It was nice you were willing to teach me. But I don't want to make you go through that much trouble."

"It's fine. I was actually kind of looking forward to it. I haven't done it in years. Besides, now that I said it, I'm looking forward to fresh fish for dinner."

I grab my keys and head back out to the car, only this time I'm followed. Mr. Darcy is right on my heels. "Nope, not a chance in hell. Get back inside." I bend down and push him towards the cabin. But he doesn't budge. "Seriously, get inside. I don't want to hit you." This time he actually sits down and looks up at me. I open the door and he comes up right next to my leg. "Fine." I grab him up and drop him on the passenger seat.

I stop at the first gas station I come to. Mr. Darcy is sitting on the passenger seat. I don't want to take him in with me so I crack a window. I'll only be a few minutes, he'll be fine. Our options are slim but it's better than dried out old bait. I grab a jar of each and head up to pay. I checkout and head back out to my car. There are about five or six people gathered around my car looking in the window. I didn't think about the kind of attraction a pig sitting in the front seat would be. They turn to me as I get to my door. A little girl looks at me, "Is that a pet pig? Can I see him? Can I pet him? Is he nice?"

"I'm sort of in a hurry." Her face falls as if I've just crushed all of her childhood dreams. I can't be the one to stand in the way of her dreams of petting a pig so I open my door and reach down and hit the unlock button, "Okay, you can pet him. But you have to be fast." Her smile is back in the blink of an eye. She opens the door and reaches in to pet him.

"Oooohhhhhhh, he is so cute! Can I get one, Mama? Can I please? I'll take real good care of it!"

A lady I'm assuming is her mother grabs her arm, "Oh no, sweetie. You can't have a pig for a pet! Where would we put it? Besides they are messy dirty animals. It's time to go."

The little girl waves as her mom drags her away from my car. The other people slowly disperse. I reach over and shut the passenger side door then put the car in reverse and head back. So much for keeping a low profile. I've got to get my focus back. I never would've been this careless. These are the types of screw ups that cost people jobs and get people killed. That's not something I'm willing to risk. I'm starting to think playing a game and going fishing isn't such a great idea. I need to distance myself from her. Somehow she's getting under my skin and I'm letting my guard down.

Pulling up to the cabin, I park the car. I take a breath and steel my resolve to distance myself from her. I open the door and grab Mr. Darcy. Imogen is up on the porch and she flies down the stairs when she spots Mr. Darcy in my arms.

"Oh thank goodness you had him!" She wraps her arms around me and the pig in my arms, "After you left I figured Mr. Darcy was just walking around the cabin but then I started calling him and he didn't come. Then I realized the door was open and I was afraid he had wandered off and was lost or dying or being eaten. But then you drove up and I saw you had him!" She drops her arms from around me and snatches the pig from my arms, "Dinner is ready."

"Sounds good, I'm starved." I can smell the spaghetti as soon as I walk in the door, "It smells delicious. Let me go wash my hands and I'll be back out." I head to the bathroom and wash my hands. I take a second to look in the mirror to give myself a pep talk, "Get it together, you can do this. You can be professional. It's a job and nothing more. Your dream is on the line."

She's already sitting at the table with the spaghetti dished up into two bowls. As soon as I sit down she dives in. Man, she can eat. It's not every day you see a girl eat real food. None of this lettuce and water shit. It's actually refreshing. I put a forkful in my mouth and it's like heaven. I can't remember the last time I had a real meal. Take out is a lot easier when there's only one of you. We finish eating at the same time and I reach for her bowl, "You cooked. I'll do the dishes."

"Thank you. I also made some cupcakes. Since you ran to the store I had extra time and it's actually Mr. Darcy's birthday and he loves cupcakes." She comes and grabs a plate of cupcakes from the counter and sets them on the table along with a tiny birthday hat that she's made. She comes back into the kitchen and reaches into the cupboard and pulls out some popcorn and kind of waves it as she says, "And I didn't forget about the popcorn I have to eat, don't worry." Then she puts it in the microwave to pop.

I'm a little distracted by the fact that she made cupcakes for her pig. "You are throwing your pig a birthday party?"

She turns to face me, "Of course not, I'm not a crazy person." I look at her skeptically. "I mean, I'm just the normal kind of crazy. I'm not crazy crazy. Besides you can't have a birthday party with only two people."

I smile at her, "The normal kind of crazy, huh?" She smiles back at me. I turn back to the dishes and I lose track of what I was about to say before the cupcakes and the pig's birthday came up. I remember, "Oh, so I was thinking," I trail off as I turn around and she already has Battleship set up and is waiting for me.

"Yes?"

She looks so excited about playing Battleship. It's like the little girl at the gas station all over again. Except, this time it isn't a little girl whose dreams I'm going to crush. It's a hot fully grown woman and one who I'm starting to feel something for. A woman with amazing strength, in spite of all she has been through. It's her whom I would be disappointing. How much can one game of Battleship hurt? In the morning I'll just say I'm sick. Or that I have more work to do. Something so we can't go fishing. Hell, maybe I'll get lucky and it'll rain.

"Mr. Darcy's growing on me." She just smiles at me. Definitely the right choice. It'll be easier tomorrow. I dump the popcorn into a bowl and sit down. I set the popcorn on the table and slide my Battleship board closer to me. My mind is already starting to strategize and I have a little rush of adrenaline. To say that I'm competitive would be putting it mildly.

After a few minutes of planning we both get our ships laid out and I grab for a cupcake. I swear everything this girl makes is heaven. The cupcake is gone in four bites and I reach for another one, "These are really good. It's a good thing I didn't have these when I came in to your café or I'd be living at the gym."

She takes one and sets it on the ground for Mr. Darcy, "Try working there every day. My self-control is really put to the test. But everything in moderation. And by moderation I mean no repeats, so, one of each."

"I didn't know pigs could eat cake. I don't know how you can do it. The smell alone would be torture. So are you going first or am I?"

"He can't have a lot of cake or have it very often, but he can have it. You can. Are we playing the normal way or Salvo rules?"

"You know how to play Salvo? I thought we were the only ones who knew that way. I don't know anyone else who plays that way."

"That's the only way June let me play growing up. She said the regular rules are for pansies and she wouldn't have me growing up to be a pansy."

"Sounds like my kind of woman." I look at my game board and try to strategize what I'm going to call out first.

I call out my five shots and don't hit anything. She follows with her five but she misses all of them as well. We call our five shots back and forth a few more times before either one of us make a hit. She ends up being the first one to hit something and the little squeal of excitement she lets out helps soften the blow. I'm surprised at how good she is. Once she got her first hit she was on fire. She seemed to know where the rest of my ships were and the rest of her calls are hits. With each sunken ship I lose one of my calls and I'm out before I even know what hit me.

I lean back in my chair and look over at her, "That is one of the only times I've lost and definitely the fastest."

"Well, it's the first time you've played me and I told you I was good," she replies with a smirk. She starts putting away the game pieces so I join in and start putting mine away. I can't even be pissed at losing with the huge grin filling her face. Things are just effortless with her. She makes it easy to forget

106

that I'm on the job and I'm here to protect her from someone trying to take her life. I grab her game board and put the game back in the box and put it back with the other games.

"I think I'm going to call it a night. If you still want to go fishing tomorrow we'll need to get an earlier start, otherwise we won't catch anything," and just like that my resolve to flake out in the morning is gone. There is no way I can disappoint her and I'm actually looking forward to it. It's been too long since I've thrown a line out.

"Oh, I didn't even think about that. And yes, I still want to go fishing tomorrow. I'll call it an early night too and be ready and raring to go in the morning. Good-night, Calder. Thanks again for a fun day."

I watch her walk to her room. The fresh air fishing will be good. It'll help clear my head. We're only here another day or so. You can't fall in love with someone in a few days. I have nothing to worry about. These feelings I think I'm getting are just attraction. They'll go away when she goes away.

CHAPTER SEVEN

- Imogen -

I wake up like a kid on Christmas. Rushing, I throw on the first clothes I grab and hurry in and make some breakfast. I'm just pulling the last two pieces of toast out of the toaster when Calder comes walking down the hall. He has on some well-worn jeans and an old ratty t-shirt. I can almost feel the drool on the side of my mouth.

"Good morning."

"Good morning," I snap out of my trance and put the toast on the plate and head to the table. "You said we needed to get an early start so I got up and started making breakfast. I wasn't sure how far we were going and if we would need to pack a lunch or not. So if we do I can make some sandwiches for us to take with us."

"We aren't going far but we'll pack lunch. Then we don't

have to cut out in the middle of fishing if we get hungry." He grabs a plate and starts eating some eggs and toast. After seeing how much he dishes up I'm thinking I should have made more. I scoop a few of the eggs that are left and half of a piece of toast and put it on a plate for Mr. Darcy. Then I take what's left and start eating.

"Okay, that sounds good. What kind of fish are out there? And do I need to be afraid of alligators?" I didn't really think about alligators when I asked to go fishing. Maybe I should have thought this through a little better. "Because you know, if there are alligators I'm pretty sure that I forgot that there was this thing I had to do today." That would be my luck. Here I've escaped death and then I get done in by an alligator.

"It's been a while since I've been fishing up here. I haven't kept up on my fish species studies," he says with a smile. I swear his eyes twinkle as he adds, "But we used to catch a lot of catfish so probably some of those. Which would be good fried for dinner. As far as alligators, they're always a possibility." I think the fear in my eyes causes him to add, "But I haven't seen one yet. And I've been coming up here for years. Plus remember it's my job to keep you safe. That means even from alligators. I'm going to go grab the fishing poles. I'll meet you out front." He sets his plate down in the sink and heads outside. Mr. Darcy and I finish eating and then I pick up our plates and take them over to the sink and clean them. Grabbing the peanut butter and the jam, I make a couple sandwiches. Thinking about this morning, I decide to make two more. Calder seems to have an empty pit for a stomach so I know they won't go to waste.

Pulling open the refrigerator door, I survey our options for drinks. I don't think beer would be appropriate even though that seems like what you're supposed to drink when fishing. I see Diet Coke and grab a couple of those. Thank goodness he's a Coke drinker too; I didn't think about telling him about my Diet Coke addiction and Pepsi would not have cut it. I put on Mr. Darcy's leash and collar that I use to walk him. I find a plastic grocery store bag that I put the sandwiches and drinks in and then head out front.

I don't see Calder out front so I head so the side of the cabin and I see him bent over looking in the shed for something. It provides the perfect opportunity to peruse his beautiful backside. His jeans are worn and fit his body perfectly. My body starts to flush and I clear my throat so I don't get caught checking someone out again.

He straightens and turns around with a baseball hat in his

hand, "Well, it's a little dusty but it should help keep the sun out of your eyes." He walks over and puts it on my head and I feel my heartbeat pick up as he gets close enough for me to smell the lingering woodsy scent of the soap he used this morning in the shower.

He steps back and I try for a playful pose, "How do I look?"

Letting out a chuckle he responds, "Great. That was my grandpa's favorite hat and I think he would like it even better on you. Let's go."

I can feel my cheeks heat up at his unexpected compliment. There's a small pathway off to the left of the shed and I follow him that way. Watching where I'm stepping so I don't trip is more work than you would think. I reach down and pick up Darcy since he's having a rougher go of it than I am. Every now and then I glance up to make sure Calder is in front of me. I smile as I see the ends of the fishing poles bouncing in tune to his steps. We finally make it to a little clearing and he sets the poles and tackle box down. Turning from left to right I take it all in. It is breathtaking. There's nothing to either side of us except trees and river. It's so peaceful and beautiful that I completely forget why I'm here, who I'm with, and that my life is so completely messed up.

"It's beautiful," I say reverently. I glance at Calder and he's smiling. The look on his face shows that this place means a lot to him.

"Thank you. This is my favorite place in the world. It's that place where I can still feel my grandma and grandpa. We spent so much time here. They loved it so much, it's almost like their spirits are in the ground and the trees. I can't believe I haven't been up here in so long. I didn't even realize I missed it."

I can sense he needs a minute and that he's a little embarrassed to let so much out, so I walk a little down the river looking around. Mr. Darcy is snorting and smelling the ground when Calder calls me back over. He's on one knee by the tackle box and is finishing putting something on the end of the fishing pole.

He stands up, "I'll cast it out for you. Watch what I do and then try to do that same after. Sound good?"

"Ummm, sure. Yes. Yes, you do it first and I'll watch." He is holding the pole and with what looks like a small flick of his wrist gets the hook out into the river. Then he reels it back in and hands it to me. Well, it didn't *look* that difficult. I take the pole from his hand and try to mimic his form and movements. But at the end of my wrist flick the hook just dumbly hangs and flips around the end of the pole.

I hear his chuckle from behind me. "That was...close. Want me to show you again?"

"Yes, please." I hand the pole back to him and watch him again. Once again he takes it and with a small flick of the wrist gets the hook to land perfectly out on the river. After he reels it in, I grab it from his hands and get my starting form right. I can feel the smile on his face at my stance before I even get to the wrist flick. I hear his laugh after I flick my wrist and once again the hook is dangling wrapped around the end of the pole.

"I'm doing exactly what you're doing. I don't know why it isn't working," I huff. I know I should cut myself some slack since this is only the second attempt at casting a fishing pole I have ever done in my life but it looks so easy. I try a few more times each with a worsening result when I hear him approach me.

"Here," he says as he grabs for the pole. He steps behind me and grabs my hand and places it on the grip at the end of the pole. Then his large warm hand envelops mine. "It's all in the angle that you let the hook go. You also have to flip the bail," he says, flipping the metal half circle thing where the line goes. Then he pulls some of the fishing line with his index finger and stretches our arms back and then brings them forward at a slight angle. When our hands are almost all the way to where we started, he lets the line go and flicks his wrist. The hook sails and lands right in the water in the shade of a tree on the other side of the bank.

I'm still trying to get my stomach to stop doing flips at the feel of my back pressed into his strong chest when I feel him let go of the pole and step back. Choosing to ignore the fact that his absence affects me, I say, "That's exactly what I was doing. Let me try it again." Not wanting to be rude I add, "Oh, and thank you."

Through his little side smile that I'm coming to look forward to seeing he replies, "Anytime. You can sit down and prop up your pole if you want. Just watch the tip every now and then. If it dips then you have a bite. I'm going to go get mine ready. I'll cast out a little bit away from you so our lines don't get crossed."

A little bummed that he isn't going to be next to me for the whole day I only manage an, "Okay." I find a couple of rocks to prop my pole up in between and sit down on a blanket that Calder surprisingly thought to grab. Mr. Darcy sprawls out next to me and enjoying the sun peeking through the leaves. I turn my head up to the sun and let the sunlight dance on my cheeks. After a few minutes I figure I should check my pole to see if I have a bite and I see Calder heading back my way. I realize his pole isn't as far away as I thought it was going to be and he actually comes and sits next to me on the blanket.

"So, how's your first fishing trip?"

"I love it! I really enjoy the outdoors and sitting out here is so peaceful. But, being completely honest, I thought it would be a little more exciting than this. It *is* fun, don't get me wrong. I guess I just always see people reeling in fish and I didn't realize how much sitting around there is."

"There's a lot of sitting around. But once we get you a fish, I promise it'll be exciting. It'll make the waiting around worth it," he awards me another one of his killer side smiles. I never would have thought when I first met him that he could even smile, let alone this much. I don't think I'll ever get sick of looking at his dimples.

"Okay, I'll be patient. So tell me about yourself. You know everything about me and I don't know anything about you. I mean, you have a whole file on me. You even knew who my dad was before I did. Even the playing field a little," I say as I nudge his shoulder.

"That seems fair. What do you want to know?"

"Well, let's start with your family. Tell me more about your brothers and sister. What do your parents do?"

"Dalton is three years younger than I am. He is a genius and is a computer programmer in New York. He's quiet and a nice guy. Justin is five years older than I am and he followed my dad's footsteps and joined the force. He's the loud, annoying one. You can dare him to do anything and he'll do it. He's still in Chicago and proposed to his girlfriend, Megan. Sarah is seven years older than I am. She lives in Chicago with her husband, Chris. They have three kids, a boy and two girls. She's funny and creative. She's an amazing artist. Her husband's on the force with Justin. My parents are still in Chicago too. My dad's a retired detective for the police department. It's sort of a family tradition. He doesn't believe in paying someone to do something that he can do himself. So I know how to do a lot of odd things. Surprisingly most of them have come in handy. He also is the first to volunteer to help someone if they need help. My mom's a homemaker. She's sweet and welcoming to everyone. I don't think anyone has a bad word to say about her. She still's holding out hope I'll go back and settle down in Chicago."

"Do you guys get along? Are you close?"

"We get along as well as any family can. We have our moments but we love each other. My parents have everyone over for dinner every Sunday. I go when I'm in town, which isn't often. I don't get many vacations and I'm kind of a workaholic so I don't leave Boston that much."

"Did you always know you wanted to join the FBI? You said your dad was a detective, right? Did he want you to follow in his footsteps?"

"Yeah, my dad was a detective. My grandpa was one too. There wasn't quite as much pressure on me to follow their footsteps since my older brother joined the force. But I always wanted to catch the bad guys, even when I was little. I just wanted to do it my own way and not have my name follow me around giving me something to live up to. I wanted to make a name for myself and not ride on my family's coattails. So the FBI was my choice. I'm about to get a promotion that will give me my pick of assignments. And I'll be smack dab in the middle of the action in Washington, D.C. Mom'll hate it, but Dad'll be proud."

"All you have to do is keep me alive," I wink.

"Something like that," he says through a chuckle. He glances at my pole and I follow his eyes and see the tip dipping down. "You've got a bite!" He jumps up and grabs my hand and pulls me up after him, "Grab your pole. Now give it a little tug to set the hook," he wraps his arms around me and places his hands on top of mine; giving the pole a quick little tug. "Then pull back a little and reel in some of the line. Nothing too drastic yet, we want to tire it out first." He starts slowing pulling the pole back and reeling in some line. He does this a few times and then he starts reeling a little faster. As the end of the line starts to get closer to the edge of the water I can see the fish.

"I did it! I caught a fish!" He laughs at my enthusiasm as he pulls the fish free of the water. It's pretty small. And by pretty I mean it would barely feed Mr. Darcy. "It's, uh, it's kind of small. I thought it would be bigger."

"That's because it's a young fish. We'll toss it back. Give it a little longer to get bigger before someone catches it again." He grabs the fish and sticks his finger in its mouth to dislodge the hook. Then he tosses the fish back out into the river. My first fish is gone just like that.

"Let's do it again!" And that's what we do. We cast out a few more times before we ended up catching anything else. Mr. Darcy wanders a little, sniffing in the bushes and leaves, but he never wanders too far. Luckily what we catch ends up being big enough to keep. After a couple hours we take a break and eat some lunch. I learn more about his nephews and niece. I can tell by the way he talks about them that he must be a great uncle and I wouldn't be surprised if he's their favorite. It's so easy to talk to him and the conversation flows. I think we're both surprised how easy it is and how much we end up sharing. I tell him about growing up with June and how much I had wished for a bigger family. He tells me about the fights and shenanigans he and his siblings got into when they were younger. After lunch I finally figured out how to cast by myself and actually caught another fish.

It's getting close to sunset when we finally decide to head back. "I'll show you how to clean and fillet them. Then we'll fry them for dinner," he says over his shoulder on our way back to the cabin.

"Oh, I guess they don't clean themselves. I didn't think about the cleaning and filleting part," I confess. My stomach starts to turn thinking about it. Thoughts of what the innards of the fish will look like are swimming in my head.

I can hear the smile in his response, "It's not too bad, I promise. It's easy and pretty quick. If you get too squeamish you can stop and I'll finish." He puts the fishing poles away while I head inside with the fish.

Inside at the kitchen sink he starts, "Now we have to skin the fish." He takes these plier clamp things and grips part of the fish right by the side fins, "We clip the side fins so we don't get poked with the spines. There's a little hard boney part. Right here. Now grab that and pull." I didn't think I had a weak stomach but when he starts pulling the skin down off of the body my stomach flips. He repeats what he just did on the other side and looks up at me. My face must betray what's happening to my stomach because he sets the fish down, washes his hands, and turns me toward the living room. "Why don't you let me finish cleaning the fish and I can make you something for a change."

I manage a slight smile and a nod and go sit on the couch with Mr. Darcy in my lap. After a few minutes my stomach calms down and I turn to watch him in the kitchen. I haven't had a guy cook for me before. It's sexy to see him in the kitchen making something for me. Thinking about how much fun I've had today I realize that I could easily get used to this. I knew I was attracted to him but the more I get to know him the more I like him..

These thoughts are more dangerous than the men he is protecting me from. His job is protecting me. He's a FBI agent. I don't know if I could be with someone who works in a job that's so dangerous. Losing someone else I care about would wreck me. I could never ask him to give up his dream. Not that he even would or we are anywhere near that point. We haven't even kissed. There's definitely something between us. I know I can't be the only one to have felt it. I'll just have to enjoy the time we have together and hope that I make it out the other side.

"It's ready."

"It smells delicious." We both sit down and start eating. "This is amazing! I can't believe we caught this and now we are eating it. Thank you so much for taking me fishing and then making this delicious dinner. If I was stuck here with anyone but you I would have gone crazy. You've kept me sane when everything in my life was turned upside down."

I see something in his eyes and I know he's going to pull away again. It had to have been something I said. Maybe I am the only one feeling something between us. His phone goes off right when he starts to say something. He stands, I hear him answer it on his way to the hall to find a good spot for reception. Leaning as far as I can without falling out of my chair, I try to listen to the conversation. I can only hear his muffled whisper and then footsteps back towards me. I'm barely sitting up straight when he gets back into the kitchen.

"That was the field office. I have to head into the office tomorrow to help with your dad's video testimonial."

"Wait, my dad is going to be here? In Louisiana?"

"No, he's in Boston. But I'll be helping them and watching via video. Also, they want us to stay here until it's safe for you to go home. They're only expecting us to be here a few more days. They didn't want to waste money and man power for a couple days when we're safe here."

"Oh, okay. So I'll just stay here tomorrow? Or do I get to go with you?"

"You'll stay here. They don't want to risk anyone seeing you. It's safer and I'll be back later in the day."

I try for as much of a smile as I can muster, "Sounds good. I'm kind of exhausted from fishing all day. I'm going to call it an early night if that's okay."

"Yeah, I was thinking the same thing actually. I need to get an early start to get into the office on time. Have a good night."

I grab Darcy and head to my room. I decide to have a quick shower before I go to bed. The water helps relax me but it also gives me time to reflect on the quick turn tonight took. Just when I start to forget why I'm here and who Calder is I'm reminded of how messed up my life is and the real reason we're here together. Maybe Calder being gone tomorrow will be good. I know I was going to enjoy the time we have together, but the more I think about it the more I know I won't be okay in the end. If I'm already starting to feel this much for him, a few more days together would have me falling hard. Why can't we just be friends? We get along great and things are easy between us. Sure he's extremely attractive but I can put that aside and we can just be friends. He's not the only hot guy that I can't have. Just my luck that two hot guys come into my life and nothing's going to happen with either of them. Heading back to my room, I've made up my mind that I can just be friends and that it'll be enough. Now if only I stick to that resolve.

- *Calder* -

I watch her go to her room and I feel deflated. We had such

an amazing day. We both shared personal stuff and were getting to know each other. She's even more amazing the more I get to know her. She's caring and is always taking care of everyone else. She's strong and brave. Then at dinner everything felt like it was shifting. People out there trying to kill her and all I can think is how badly I want to grab her in my arms and make her forget everything and everyone but the two of us. There's no possible way things could work. Her life and family are here and mine's in Boston and hopefully soon to be in D.C. I know the facts but I can't explain the way my heart fell knowing I don't get to spend tomorrow with her. Our time is limited and I was looking forward to having another whole day with her.

Something changed after that phone call. She pulled away and I can't say that I blame her. There's something between us and it has the possibility to completely destroy us both. Or it could end up being what people write about and fight wars over. I'm not sure I'm ready for that. I've got to put my feelings aside and not let things get out of control. Things need to stay professional. I can't and I won't be the thing that ruins her. She's dealt with shit and come out stronger and braver than anyone should be. I can't risk starting something that I can't finish.

I clean up dinner and hear her start the shower. After

everything I've just decided about how we can't start anything and things need to stay professional, my mind takes a very unprofessional route. I'm imagining things that have me gripping the counter to keep me from going to her. Closing my eyes I can see the water droplets caressing her skin. One water droplet is making its way down her neck and then down her collar bone. Before I can finish watching it completing its journey to the drain, the water shuts off and I'm jolted out of my fantasy.

My breathing is heavy and I have to compose myself at the sink before I move. I think I hear her go back into her room but I can't risk her seeing me like this. After I've gotten myself in control I head to my room hoping to run into her. But she's back in her room with the door shut. Passing the bathroom I can feel the warmth and steam from her shower on my skin. It only serves to increase my desire for her.

Memories of the day invade my mind as I try to fall asleep. Seeing her in my grandpa's hat was the tipping point. Something changed in me and I'm not sure what. All I know is I felt it then and now just reliving the memory. The huge smile on her face when she caught her first fish. Sunlight playing with the freckles on her cheeks as she tells me about growing up with June. Even that damn pig makes it into my mental replay. My last thought before sleep finally takes me is that keeping my distance from Imogen is going to be a lot easier said than done.

CHAPTER EIGHT

- Imogen -

The next morning I purposefully stay in my room until after Calder has left. He stopped by my door and told me if I was awake that I might want to stay inside since it looked like it was going to storm at some point today. I didn't say anything. It actually really irritated me if I'm honest. Who does he think he is to tell me what to do? I can go outside if I want to go outside. In fact, I love the rain.

My irritation gets the better of me and helps push me into deciding to try fishing on my own. There won't be a more opportune time to perfect my fishing skills than while he's gone. I'll be able to practice all day without having to worry about him judging me or offering to help me by wrapping me in his arms and pressing his body against mine. My mind will be focused. I'll be a well oiled fishing machine by the time he gets back.

After I make some breakfast, I grab a snack and head out to the shed for a fishing pole and the tackle box. Since I'm a novice I'm not sure what all I need to bring but I figure I'm probably covered if I bring a pole and the tackle box he had yesterday. Mr. Darcy and I make our way back to the same spot we were yesterday. Today there isn't any sunlight dancing through the leaves and everything seems quiet. The birds aren't as loud as they were yesterday and even the river seems hunkered down, ready for the storm. I get a little uneasy at the thought of getting stuck out here in the middle of a storm but I came all the way here I'm going to fish for at least an hour or two. Besides I have to stay and prove Calder wrong.

Time goes by slowly, especially since I don't get any bites. My casting is getting better so I guess the time wasn't a complete waste. Packing up and getting ready to head back, I notice Mr. Darcy sniffing in a bush a little too close to the water for comfort. Rushing to the worst case scenario that there's probably an alligator in the bush ready to eat my baby, I run over and whip him away from it. When nothing jumps out at me I use my foot to move the bush to try and see what was holding his attention. That's when I see the cutest, fluffiest, and tiniest little duckling. Since I'm no longer afraid an alligator is going to eat Mr. Darcy, I set him down and move closer to the duckling.

At first I assume its mother is just around the corner and is probably holding back since I'm here. But then I realize it's odd that there would only be one duckling and not more if the mother was really just hiding out of sight. Well, that and mother ducks aren't known for hiding from people when they think their ducklings are in danger. In fact, they are usually pretty aggressive and she would probably be here quacking at me to leave her baby alone. Bending down, I grab the duckling before it can scuttle away from me. I'm not an expert on ducklings but I'm assuming this one is probably only a week old. I can't leave this tiny little duckling out here all on its own. There might not have been a threat yet but I know there are alligators out here and even just this storm could be dangerous for a duckling this tiny.

I grab Mr. Darcy in one arm so he doesn't slow me down and I hold the fishing pole under the other. The duckling is cradled in my hand as I turn towards the cabin.

I hurry back as fast as I can to beat the storm but carrying a pig, duckling, fishing pole, and tackle box is awkward. I should have just left the fishing stuff there and then gone back and gotten it. But I didn't want Calder to be mad since this stuff has sentimental value to him. Not taking the time to put everything away where I grabbed it, I just set it inside the shed and shut the door.

Once inside, I set Mr. Darcy down and try to think what I'm going to do with the duckling. I don't even know what to feed it. I do know that you aren't supposed to give ducklings bread. Trying to think of anything I could use to feed it, I remember seeing some rescue show where they said in an emergency you could give baby ducks a mixture of oats and cornmeal made into a little crumble. It's better than nothing I guess. When Calder gets back I can have him look online for what ducklings eat. If he hadn't confiscated my phone then I would be able to look myself. I'd forgotten he had taken my phone. Funny how something that seemed like such a necessity was easily forgotten once I was having fun with him.

I notice the duckling has pooped on my hand. Not wanting to set it on the ground in case it does it again I take it into the bathroom with me to wash my hands. Inspiration strikes when I see the bathtub. Filling the bathtub up with a little bit of lukewarm water I put the duckling in there and it immediately starts to swim around.

"All right, little duck, we've got to give you a name." Looking at the duckling swimming around, I try to decide if it's a girl or a boy; this young they all look the same. I decide she's a she. "You look like a Cleo. So Cleo it is."

Cleo is darker than most ducklings I've seen. She has a black beak and is mostly a dark brownish black color. Her face fades to a lighter brownish yellow color around her eyes and her belly is whiter with a few white spots along her wings. I leave her to swim while I go and get her some food and water and try to find a box or something she can sleep in.

After looking as much as I dare I don't find anything that will work. I'll have to use a towel until Calder gets back and can look in the basement and the shed. I realize after getting some oats that we don't have cornmeal but that since you mix the cornmeal with the oats that just oats probably won't kill it. After mixing it with a little bit of water to make it sort of crumbly I put it on a small plate and put some water in another one. Grabbing Cleo out of the bathtub and wrapping her up in the towel I sit on the floor and set her down in front of the food and water. Mr. Darcy comes to see what we're doing. Once he realizes he isn't getting any of Cleo's food he leaves.

Cleo eats a little bit of the food and then waddles back to the towel. I wrap her up and head into the living room. Dropping down on the couch Mr. Darcy hops up and cuddles Cleo and me.

Startling awake I realize I fell asleep. Cleo is still sleeping in the towel and Mr. Darcy is still curled up in my lap. Thinking if I was Cleo I might need to relieve myself again and not knowing a better place for her to go I decide to put her back in the bathtub. I lie back down on the couch and doze off again.

- Calder -

Today was exhausting. I'm just looking forward to getting back to Imogen and relaxing. My resolve to keep my distance is fading fast. I pull into the driveway and park. She's asleep on the couch and I don't want to wake her. I've got to piss so I head to the bathroom in the hall. I'm zipping up my pants when I hear something coming from the bathtub. It sounds a little like water splashing which doesn't make any sense since the only other person here is asleep on the couch. Training kicks in and I whip my gun out and fling the curtain open. Never in a million years would I expect to see what I saw in the bathtub. When I replay what happened next I can think of a thousand ways I could have handled it better.

I blame my reaction on my adrenaline. After my heart returns to a semi normal rhythm I start to get pissed. "IMOGEN!" I leave the duck swimming in the bathtub and stomp out to the living room. "IMOGEN!"

She's scrambling off of the couch as I get to the living room. There must be enough anger showing on my face because I

132

can visibly see her gulp. I take a breath before I carefully say every word, "Care to tell me why there is a duck swimming in my bathtub?"

"Um, well, I uh, I was hoping to do this in a better way but I guess that chance is out the window," she's wringing her hands together in front of her stomach. "So I was bored and decided to go and try fishing. I figured I could practice casting since you were gone and there wasn't much of anything else to do. I didn't catch anything if you were wondering. But my casting did get a lot better. Anyway I was just getting ready to head back so I wouldn't get caught in the storm. Is it storming yet? Never mind, let me finish. So I was getting ready to head back and Mr. Darcy was snorting and sniffing a bush. At first I was scared it was an alligator so I hurried and grabbed him but when nothing came out to eat us I decided to look in the bush. That's when I saw Cleo. I looked to see if I could see any more ducklings or her mom or anything but she was all by herself and I couldn't leave her out there for an alligator to eat or to die in the storm so I brought her back here."

"Cleo? You gave it a name? I'm not sure what I'm angriest about. The fact that you went out on your own where you could get lost or anyone could find you. Or who knows what. Or that there is currently a duck swimming in my bathtub. Get your shoes on we're going to go put it back. You're not keeping it."

She hurries and gets shoes on and then grabs a towel and grabs the duck. Great now I'll have to throw that towel away. It probably has duck shit on it.

"I'll go and look and see if we can see her mom but, Calder, I promise I looked around and waited for a while and never saw any other ducks."

"Well, we'll put it back and it'll find its way home."

She straightens her back and her face narrows as she responds, "You are out of your mind if you think I'm leaving a helpless duckling out by a river full of alligators. I'll humor you and go and see if we can find her mom. But if we don't find her - and we won't because I'm not an idiot; I wouldn't steal a duckling from the wild if it wasn't going to die without me - then Cleo is coming back with us or I'm not going anywhere."

I growl and I stomp out the door. "Fine! Hurry, we might be able to make it there and back before the storm hits. Knowing your penchant for finding trouble we'll probably be struck by lightning." She follows behind me. I'm not sure if it's the fresh air or the walk back to the river but I've calmed down by the time we get there. I start to regret what I said and how I acted. But I've got to stick to my guns. I've already got a pig staying in my cabin. There isn't any room for a duck. A duck, only Imogen would find an orphaned duck in the few hours she's by herself.

"Where did you find it?" I start to feel sprinkles of rain as soon as we get to the river.

"Her. I found *her* over here in this bush," she gestures to a bush near the river. We start looking around for any signs of any other ducks. The rain just keeps coming harder and harder. We've been looking for only about fifteen minutes when it really picks up. I look at the duck nestled in the towel in her arms. As much as I protested I'm not some heartless monster. I knew we wouldn't be leaving the duck here any more than we would have left the pig.

"We've got to get back. You can keep the duck. If I see poop in the cabin even once, it's gone."

"Thank you! I promise she won't poop on the floor and I'll clean up after her."

We both start jogging back to the cabin. By the time we get back we are soaking wet and cold. I grab a couple of clean dry towels and hand one to her. We try in vain to dry ourselves and get warm but it's the type of storm that soaks you to the bone. "I'm going to hop in the shower to warm up. You should probably do the same."

"Oh yes, that sounds amazing."

We both head to take warm showers. Not wanting to steal her warm water I wait until after I hear her water stop to take mine. I haven't been in there for more than five minutes when the power goes out. As soon as it blinks off fear grips me. What if I was followed back here? For the second time today, training takes over. Leaping out of the shower, I grab my gun and run into the hall.

I've barely made it a few steps before I smack into and fall on top of someone. Her chest is rising and falling rapidly. Lifting myself up on my forearms, I try to lift my weight off of her. As my eyes adjust, I see her staring into my eyes. Her eyes dart down to my lips and then back up to my eyes.

"I, I think I blew a fuse," she says barely above a whisper. My brain realizes that there isn't a threat at the same time my body realizes she is in no more than a tank top and shorts and I'm completely naked. And I'm on top of her. Our bodies are pressed together and I can feel every inch by smooth warm inch of her.

I remember she said something. "I was afraid I was followed and someone had cut the power." Our breaths are both coming fast and hard. It's no longer adrenaline causing our heavy breathing but combined desire and attraction. Searching her face and not finding any protest I can't fight it anymore. Locking my eyes with hers, I lower my mouth to capture hers. My tongue dives into her mouth. As soon as I taste her I completely lose control.

Her hand slides up my arm and grips my shoulder. The bite of her nails into my skin only helps to loosen my control. I roll my weight to my one arm and with my free hand reach up and hold her head to mine. She arches up and into my body. Just when I start to slide my hand down her neck we both feel and hear the snorting from Mr. Darcy. His snorts and cold nose pressed against our arms jolt us back to reality. Looking into my eyes, she starts to giggle. Then her giggle turns into a laugh that has her tilting her head back and just like that I start laughing. Soon we are both laughing. I rest my forehead against her forehead.

I go to stand up and remember I am completely naked, "I don't have any clothes on." She smirks as she raises her hand to cover her eyes. Relishing the feel of her body beneath mine for a few more seconds, I finally lift myself off of her and head back into my room to get some clothes on.

After I am dressed I grab a flashlight from the nightstand next to my bed and head back out to the hall. I don't see her in the hall so I yell out, "The breaker box is down in the basement. I'll be right back."

I go down and see the blown fuse. Flipping the switch solves the problem and I see light pouring through the door and down the stairs. She's sitting on the couch when I get into the living room. She stands as she sees me and her cheeks flush. We both start to talk at the same time and then we both let out a breath. I pause, waiting for her to start.

"I'm sorry about the fuse. I guess I had too many things plugged in."

"It's fine. Really. The wiring is old and it happens a lot." Things are a little awkward. We stand there looking at each other.

"Since we're keeping Cleo, we need to figure out what ducklings eat. I couldn't Google it since you took my phone, but I figured you could look it up."

"There are a few pet stores in town. I'm sure they'll have something or will at least know where we should look. We can head in tomorrow and then stop at the grocery store to stock back up."

"Oh that would be perfect! There are a few things I was needing and it would be nice to be able to pick them up," she trails off. She looks to be steeling herself before she continues, "About what happened."

I come around the couch to her. "Imogen, I'm not sure what this is between us. I'm not even sure how or if it will work. I do know that I've really enjoyed the last few days. And I really enjoyed what just happened. I don't want this to be awkward or try to define this. Especially since I don't think either of us really know what's going on here. What I really want is to continue to get to know you and keep having fun. Whatever happens at the end of this, we can figure it all out."

She shyly walks over to me, "I agree. We should take advantage of the time we have together." She rises up on her toes to press a kiss on my lips. I wrap my arms around her and pull her into me. I deepen the kiss until I feel a gentle push on my chest. Not wanting to pull away but also not wanting to push her too far too fast I pull back and rest my forehead against her head. We both exhale and smile at each other.

"We haven't eaten dinner. I was thinking about making a sandwich. Do you want one?"

A sandwich isn't what I'm craving right now. "Sure. That sounds great." She heads into the kitchen and I follow her to help. Her lips turn up into a smile when she notices me following her. We turn out to be an awesome sandwich making team. If sandwich making was an Olympic event we would take the gold. Before we eat she goes and checks on the duck. She gets it and Mr. Darcy settled and then she sits across from me at the table.

She asks how things went with her dad today. I tell her as much as I can. We were able to get his video testimony. It'll be used in the case against Manuel Rodriguez. The judge will be getting it and watching it tomorrow. She seems to want to ask more questions but settles for starting to eat her sandwich. In between bites of sandwich we get to know each other even more. We start with the basics like favorite color and favorite food. Then we move onto the important stuff like favorite sports team. After we finish our sandwiches we keep talking. I've never gotten to know someone like this. Michelle was my one and only serious relationship and that ended two years ago. I've never been big into commitment. My job is my priority. It's always been about getting to D.C. and out in the field. Things have always been easy. I knew where my life was going and what my next step was. For the first time in my life, I'm starting to second guess that. I'm excited at the prospect of the unknown.

We lose track of time while we talk. It isn't until we both are yawning in between words that I glance at my watch. "It's getting late. We should get to bed. We'll head into town early. Hopefully we can get in and out before it starts to get busy. The less chance of you being seen the better."

When we get to her door we pause and turn towards each other. She leans against her door and looks up at me. Looking into her eyes, I'm at a loss at what to say. I feel like I need to apologize for earlier but I don't know how. This day has been a ringer. I went from exhausted to fuming angry to afraid and ready to kill to raging desire.

"Well, this is me."

"I had fun with you today. Even if you did bring in an orphaned duck and put it in my bathtub."

"I said I was sorry for that. Besides you can't really have expected me to leave her out there. She'd probably be dead if I left her out there." She is starting to get worked up again.

"Hey, I was joking. And no, you couldn't have left her." At the look she gives me I add, "Cleo. You couldn't have left Cleo out there by herself. You have the biggest heart of anyone I know. It's one of the things I like about you. Besides she's kind

141

of growing on me." She smiles at that statement. "Well, I guess I should get to bed."

"Good-night."

We both hesitate for a second before we lean into each other. This kiss is different than the ones earlier. There's desire behind this kiss but there's else, like a promise of more. "I'll see you in the morning."

She opens her door and smiles as she shuts it. I head to my room and lay on my bed. Sleep eludes me for a while. My mind is spinning but none of the thoughts have any direction. It seems like hours before I finally fall asleep.

CHAPTER NINE

- Imogen -

This morning we had a quick breakfast and then decided to head into town. In the hopes of trying to be quick we decided to leave Mr. Darcy and Cleo at the cabin. Cleo is locked in the bathroom in the bathtub with some food, water and a towel. Mr. Darcy is locked in my room with his litter box and a blanket. Hopefully we'll get back and the cabin will still be in one piece. It's hot and humid after the storm yesterday. My white t-shirt is sticking to me and the air conditioner in the car feels like heaven.

Calder turns the radio on to a classic rock station. "I didn't take you for a classic rock type of guy, rap or country maybe. Although you're from Chicago so I guess rock makes more sense."

"Country? Definitely not country. I don't mind some rap."

"You just sort of look like the All-American boy next door so country seemed right." I mutter under my breath, "Boy next door, with a body of a Greek god."

The drive into town is silent but comfortable. We decide to stop by the pet store first. It's a little local mom and pop type store. Unfortunately they don't have what we need. They were really helpful though and told us that the Petsmart would have some duck food. It's farther in the city and on the other end which makes Calder nervous. He doesn't want to drive farther into the city; he wants to stay out on the edge of town.

"Maybe it's better to go somewhere bigger and that's busy. Then someone is less likely to be able to pick me out of a crowd. Plus we don't have much of a choice. Cleo needs to eat and we have to feed her the right kind of food."

"I'm not happy about it and if my supervisors find out I'll probably be fired," he glances at me and graces me with one of his one sided grins I'm coming to love and adds, "Although if they found out about most of my actions at the cabin I'd probably be fired."

My blood starts to heat, my cheeks flush, and I squeeze my legs together when I think about yesterday. He chuckles at my discomfort. The easy banter between us gives me the courage to ask, "So I was wondering if there was any way I could have my phone. Just to check my messages or check in. June and Kelly are probably worried sick since I haven't touched based with them at all. Plus I'm stressing about my shop and what if there was an emergency?" I start to ramble a little when he doesn't say anything at first.

"No. It's out of the question. Besides I don't even have your phone with me. It's back at the cabin. We only have a few more days of this and then you can go home. Plus, didn't you tell them I was stealing you away for a, what did you call it? A 'sexcation'?" My ears burn when he reminds me of what I called our pretend getaway. The fact that he remembers makes what I'm going to do later a little more embarrassing than it already was. He continues, "If I really did take you away on a sexcation, you wouldn't have any time to check in."

At that my stomach flips and I want so badly for it to be true. Just a few more hours and hopefully it will be. I never thought of myself as easy, I mean I'm no saint, but I don't just hop into bed with every guy who looks my way. But the thoughts going through my head and the tingles spreading throughout my body just at his words help reaffirm my decision. I have no response to his words and he knows it. We keep stealing glances at each other on the drive. A teenage girl is probably less giddy than I am right now.

When we get to Petsmart, we both head in and I excuse myself to the bathroom. If he won't give me my phone I'll find one to use. There can't be any harm in checking in real fast. I head to the grooming department and ask to use their phone. They seem skeptical so I tell them I'm just checking to see where my husband is and that we are supposed to be meeting here to drop our dog off. I'm proud of my quick, brilliant, albeit pretty transparent lie as she hands me the phone. I'm pretty sure I hear her mutter whatever under her breath. Maybe it wasn't skepticism I was sensing but the fact that I was making her work. Oh well, I don't care, I'm on a mission. The thrill of doing something I'm not supposed to do is making me giggly.

I decide to try Kelly first since she was who I talked to when I first left with Calder. Deciding not to bother her at the café and avoid a barrage of questions, I call her house phone. There isn't any risk of someone answering since she is covering for me and I know Ben will be busy at work. I try to leave it short and to the point but with enough detail that she doesn't get suspicious. Hopefully she can understand my half muffled whispered voicemail. I didn't want to blow my cover. Not wanting to take too long and run the risk of Calder catching me, I forgo calling June. Kelly was supposed to let her know where I was and knowing June she is probably off skydiving or has dragged Mabel to some rock concert.

Looking down various aisles I finally find him with a bag of duck and goose food. Man, he is drool worthy. It's almost like he is a cliché from one of the romance novels I love to read. He smiles when he sees me and we head to the checkout together. After he pays, my stomach growls and I notice I'm getting a little hungry so I ask if we can swing through and get some fast food. There's a McDonald's right by Petsmart that he grudgingly takes me to. He doesn't order anything and after eating I'm not sure the burger was worth the lecture I got about how bad fast food is for me and the disgusted look I got the whole time I ate. Never mind, Big Macs are always worth it.

Calder decides that the grocery store closer to the cabin is better. It's smaller and there isn't as much foot traffic. So his reasoning is it's safer and it's on the way and then the food won't be out of the refrigerator for as long. For some reason he seems to be pretty urgent to get back to the cabin. I'm not complaining since I'm looking forward to trying to seduce him later. We've both agreed to enjoy the time we have left and that time is getting shorter. Besides he's hot and no one will blame me.

He parks right in front of the store and we head in. I let him push the cart and we start to gather the items on our list. Three boxes of Pop Secret join our cart and he laughs at me. His urgency to get back to the cabin has lessened as we meander through the grocery store. We go up and down each aisle and we take turns tossing in things we want or need. I grab a bottle of wine and he silently raises his eyebrows as I set it in the cart. Now's the part I've been dreading. I have no idea how I'm going to get away from him to get what I need. Since I'm planning on seducing him later I have to be prepared. My traitor of a body almost gives me away as I say, "I, um, I have to go grab something. I'll be right back."

He responds with a casual smile, "I'll go with you."

"No," I rush out, "It's, a, I'm, a, I need to get some feminine products." By now my whole face is flaming red. Great, so not only am I going to pick out some condoms that I just realized he is going to have to pay for since I don't have my wallet but now he thinks I'm on my period.

"Oh, okay. Well, I'll just be over in the deli I guess." He turns and leaves me standing in the aisle like an idiot. I turn to try and find the aisle I want. I've gone past all of the aisles at least twice before I finally find the aisle I want. Glancing around to see if anyone is watching me I look at the condoms. Geez, how many different kinds and brands are there? While I like my new empowered female persona I don't have the knowledge to pull this off. I've never had to deal with buying these before. The guy always had them or it didn't happen. There are different sizes? Five minutes pass as I stand just staring at the shelves. Screw it, I'll just grab some of all of them. I smile when I realize I know what he felt like looking at the popcorn. Once he sees what I have, he probably won't be doing much thinking if you know what I mean. Chuckling to myself at my joke, I go to find him and bump into someone at the beginning of the aisle.

"Imogen?"

It takes a minute to recognize him since he is so out of place here. The shock of seeing someone familiar bursts my little bubble of non-reality. "Michael? What in the world are you doing here?" Realizing what I'm holding, I try to hide the packs of condoms behind my back but he wraps me up in a huge hug. The whirlwind of the last couple days and all the chaos hits me a little as I am enveloped in familiar arms. I squeeze him back with my one free arm.

"Girl, have I missed you! Where have you been, slut? You fell off the face of the earth. I had to get ready for that fundraiser all by myself. I'm not sure I can ever forgive you for bailing on me."

"Oh that's right! I totally forgot! I'm so sorry, Michael. You might forgive me once you find out why." I wiggle my eyebrows and my mouth breaks into a huge smile. I stick to the story I told Kelly, just in case she's talked to him, "I'm actually with a guy."

"A guy? Tell me, tell me, tell me! Wait, you're not seeing anyone."

"Well, that's the thing, I've sort of been on a couple dates with Wall Street."

"Girl, how dare you hold out on me! I want all the juicy details. *Please* tell me there are juicy details. Is he here? Do I finally get to see this sex on a stick you and Kelly are always talking about?"

He grabs me by the arm and starts dragging me towards the front entrance of the store. His fingers start to cut into my arm a little bit and the sting of his nails breaking skin have me on edge. I try to pull my arm out of Michael's grasp but can't. "Michael! Michael you are hurting me." He loosens his grip a little but doesn't let go.

"Sorry. I just don't want to miss seeing Wall Street. You guys have been going on and on about him. I've felt left out. Now I can finally see him! I guess I should know his real name. I can't be calling him Wall Street forever."

"Actually his name is Brett and he's here in the store. We can go find him so you can check him out," I grab his hand and loop my arm through his to try to avoid the digging of his nails in to my arm again. "So how did the fundraiser event go? Did you hook up with that artist you were talking about?"

"You wouldn't even believe it! That's actually why I'm still hanging around here. The fundraiser was at the Brunner Gallery and Justin, the featured artist, just lives right around the corner. Obvi, we hit it off at the fundraiser and so I've been staying with him. And by staying with him I mean we haven't left the bed for two days. I'm lucky to have slipped out to come here." He keeps glancing over his shoulder and picking up the pace a little. Something seems a little off or hurried. Turning his head forward he whispers to me, "Imogen, I think there's someone following us. I think we should leave. You can call Brett from my car."

My heart drops. They found me. I'm straining my neck as I look all around trying to find Calder. I need him. "Michael,

I have to find Calder." At the panic in my voice he slows and looks at me.

"Calder? Who's Calder? I thought you said you were with Wall Street or Brett or whatever."

He's still slowly pulling me to the door when my eyes catch Calder's. He's at the back of the store making his way up to me. He pauses when he sees me with someone. Michael turns looks where I'm looking. When Calder sees him, his face wrinkles with confusion for second. Almost in the way you do when you recognize someone but can't place their face. Confusion is replaced with fear as he yells my name, "Imogen! Run!"

None of this is making any sense. I'm trying to understand why Calder is saying what he's saying and Michael pulling me outside in the opposite direction of Calder is angering and distracting me. All I know is that I need to get to Calder. "Michael. Michael! Stop, I need to get to Calder."

"Immy, someone's following us. We have to get to my car."

"That's Calder. I have to get to him. He'll keep us safe and then I can explain everything to you." As we are almost to a grey sedan, Calder comes rushing out of the store. He has his phone up to his ear and his gun out. What happens next leaves me breathless. I don't know how or why or what but as soon as I see him ice runs through my veins. His face is a mask of helplessness, fear, and anger. "Michael. Michael, let me go. Let me go now," I'm turning away from him and trying to pull my arm out of his grasp. My mind can't process anything right now. I'm barely able to register the motion of his right arm coming up. I see the flash of sun reflect off of something and then I hear a gunshot quickly followed by another gunshot. "No!" I scream as I turn to see Calder fall. My arm reaches fruitlessly to him. Anger makes my blood boil and my survival instincts kick in and take over.

I start hitting and kicking and anything I can do to try to get away. Michael's strength is deceiving. The way he acts and looks you would think that he is thin and therefore pretty weak. All I feel when he wraps his arms around me and lifts me up is hard sinewy muscle. With one last burst of adrenaline I start flailing. When that again proves to be pointless, I realize I still have the condoms in my hands I try to throw them at Michaels face. Maybe I can get lucky enough to hit him in the eye, anything I can to try to get him to drop me so I have a fighting chance of getting to Calder. I'm not sure exactly where he was hit but that fact he is still down and I saw the left side of him kick back is not encouraging.

Helplessly I watch as I'm pulled farther and farther away from Calder. My mind and body have gone numb as I feel the burning metal of a car sitting in the sun on my leg. The heat of the metal sends fire to my resolve to fight. My mind's still refusing to process that this is Michael doing this. I can't even start on the why of it. Shock mixed with adrenaline has my mind spinning in a million different directions. Half of me is still hoping this is some horrible misunderstanding. When Michael turns me to face him, the look on his face is all I need to see to know this is not a misunderstanding. His eyes are devoid of any emotion. His movements are calculated and thoroughly planned out. Like a big cat stalking its prey. A paralyzing wave of fear has me immobile. We stare at each other for what feels like eternities. His lips turn into an amused smirk right before I feel the butt of his gun come crashing into my temple. Everything goes black.

- *Calder* -

I'm not sure why Imogen didn't want me to come with her to pick up the stuff she needed. It would take more than some tampons and pads to make me uncomfortable. Growing up with my sister, I've seen my fair share of girlie products. But the slightly panicky embarrassed look on her face has me turning the cart away and leaving her.

154

She seems to have been gone for a while. I've almost memorized all of the drinks on the shelves when the little curl of fear that has been in my stomach since we left the pet store grows. This is too long. She shouldn't have been gone this long. Almost annihilating an old lady with my cart I start towards the aisle she should be down. She isn't there but I think I see the ends of her hair whipping around the end of the aisle. Hurriedly I'm jogging with the cart along the back of the store looking down the aisles just trying to get a glimpse of her and see that she's okay. Fear is morphing into panic with each empty aisle.

Finally I get to the end of the aisles to the produce section. There's a clear view of the front of the store. I spot Imogen with a well-dressed man who looks to be very into his appearance. His hair is in a wave on top of his head, like the guys in those fashion magazines. He is in tight khaki pants and a suit coat. Way overdressed for the supermarket in my opinion. Imogen sees me as I pause trying to figure out who she could be with. The guy who is holding her arm turns around. His face looks familiar and I'm trying to place him. I know I know him from somewhere. When his eyes meet mine, I can feel dread in the pit of my stomach. There is nothing in their depths except icy cool determination. That's when it clicks. I know where

I've seen him and the realization does nothing to dispel the dread coursing through my body. No one really knows who he is. He's like a ghost. He shows up right when someone goes missing or turns up dead. No evidence. No clues. I'm not sure how I manage but my lips open and I shout, "Imogen! Run!"

Confusion washes over her face at my words. He starts pulling her out the door and away from me. I'm racing after them as my right hand reaches behind me for my gun and my left hand has my phone out dialing. As I rush out into the sunlight I manage a few words to the person on the other end of the phone, "Agent Calder, Imogen's gone." I don't have a clear shot of him. The glint of sun off of the barrel of his gun is all the warning I get. I'm not quite fast enough and the shot slams into my left shoulder. The impact knocks my phone out of my arm. He's still pulling Imogen away from me. There's still not a clear shot and with the pain of the hit to my shoulder I'm afraid I'll hit Imogen even if there was. His gun goes off again and this time I feel it tear into my thigh. The force combined with the pain from both shots has me falling to the ground. I watch helplessly as he drags her and starts taking her to the back of a car. Suddenly there are boxes flying but they do little to stop him. He gets her to the back of a car and knocks her out and shoves her in the trunk. My fingers curl around my phone as dots start forming in my eyes from the pain of being shot and reaching for my phone. I bite out a few words into the phone, "Agent down. Suspect at large. Charge taken." Then the blackness takes me.

CHAPTER TEN

- Imogen -

I'm first aware of the tight burning sensation in my shoulders and chest. Next the throbbing pain in my head and behind my closed eyelids rears its ugly head. With every heartbeat the pressure in my head throbs, causing my eyes to water. Confused as to why I'm in so much pain, I try to open my eyes. All I manage to accomplish is to blink a few times and let out a breathy grunt. As my mind's coming into focus I come to the conclusion that I'm sitting in a chair and my arms are tied behind my back. I know my hands are behind my back, and have been for a little while based off of the puffiness in my hands and fingers. It feels like tiny pins and needles are poking my hands and fingers but the pooling of blood has caused a numbing effect so it's more annoying than painful.

"Good morning, sunshine! It's about time you woke up. I

barely hit you and you've been out for hours. I was afraid I had killed you but I could see you breathing and I kept checking your pulse. That would *not* have been good. They need you alive, at least for right now. I've been so bored waiting for you to wake up."

My heart plummets to my feet when I hear his voice. My mind is flooded with the memories of the events that lead to me being tied in this chair. Fear and panic wash over me. Shiny brown leather shoes step into my line of sight and the pants attached to those shoes bend. A face that used to make me laugh peeks into view. Hands that have held me through tears grab my knees. I shudder at the sensation that brings and nausea rolls through my stomach. The sides of his mouth kick up and before I can stop myself I spit out, "Why are you doing this? I thought we were friends!" Tears are flowing freely and the new sting of his betrayal puts the rest of the pain out of my mind. There is no stopping the words and thoughts spilling out of my mouth. "Who are you?" I whisper as I choke on the sobs wracking my body. I try to bring my crying under control. Tears won't be of any use to me here. After a couple deep breaths I glance up.

He stands and starts to walk away from me. I use this opportunity to look around and try to get a feel for where I am. Helplessness envelopes me as I glance around a large open room. I'm not trained for this. I don't know what time it is or where I am. I never should have been so cavalier about this. It was easy to joke about when Calder was with me. He made me feel safe. He tried to tell me how serious it was but it still didn't sink in. I look back up at Michael and another wave of nausea hits my stomach. To think that someone I trusted and cared for could do something so evil. Tears spring from my eyes again as the image of Calder falling replays in my mind. I've got to try to pull it together. I might not know what to do to get myself out of this, but I can't just sit here and let him do whatever he wants to me. I go through every movie I've ever seen about kidnapping or escaping. If only my dad was Liam Neeson then I wouldn't have to worry.

Looking around I try to take in as much detail as possible, not that I know if it will help at all. I doubt there is going to be a glowing exit sign. I'm guessing it's around dusk since there isn't much light and the windows are tinted pinkish orange. It looks like I'm in the middle of an abandoned warehouse or something like that. I'm in one big room. There are windows high along the left wall, too high for any hope of climbing through them. It's been abandoned for a while. The grime coating the windows looks years thick and there are broken panes in at least four of the windows. My shoes slide easily along on the floor thanks to the layer of dust and dirt. That won't help in a getaway attempt. Knowing my luck, I'll probably slip and fall and kill myself for him. From what I can see there seems to be what looks like an office towards the far right end of the room. There's another small room next to that and I think I can make out a small sink so it's probably safe to say that that's a bathroom. That's about all I can make out. I'm not hearing car horns or dogs barking. In fact it's eerily quiet. From my review of movies that probably means we are in the middle of nowhere. Isn't that usually what the killers do? Take you miles away from anywhere useful. So even if I managed to get out of the warehouse I would be wandering around outside with no way to get anywhere. Then he'd just kill me out there. He starts talking and my attention is pulled back to him.

"Well, you know mostly who I am. What you don't know is that I have a certain set of skills." At his reference to the movie *Taken,* he giggles. His reference makes me shiver and I'm disgusted that we watched that movie together cuddled up on my couch. The fact that we both thought of that movie makes me sick. "I've always wanted to say that. Actually, I'm a hit man. Although that title is so blah. I need something snazzy. You know how I love abbreviations so what about C.E.O., chief extermination officer." He laughs at his own joke and continues, "No, that's ew. It's not exciting at all. I'll have to keep thinking about it. Any who, I was hired to watch you and wait. This has actually been longer than most of my other jobs so that's fun. I settled myself into your life and decided to have a little fun. Then a few days ago I got the order to take you. Not take you out, not yet at least. And well, here we are."

"So everything's been a lie? It was all fake?" My heart hurts to hear that our friendship has all been a lie, a ruse to get close to me and get me to trust him.

"Oh honey, you can't fake this much fabulousness. It's brilliant really, the perfect cover. Who would suspect a gay artist to be a hit man? Everyone *loves* a gay best friend," he pauses almost like he is waiting for me to agree. When I don't he continues, "No, the hit man thing came later. My artistic talent was evident at a young age. That's how they noticed me. It just so happened that my skills weren't limited to paint and canvas. I was in a group home and one day a man and a woman came and took me. I was always getting in trouble. Pesky morals and emotions never held me back from getting what I wanted. They were just happy to get to rid of me so they gave me to the first person to come looking. I was the perfect student and a quick learner. I actually made my first kill by my sixteenth birthday. Oh well, enough about me." To add insult to injury he adds, "To answer your question, obvi I faked the friendship. I'm such an amazing actor. It's really kind of sad. You were so desperate for friendship you didn't even question anything."

I have no idea why he told me his whole life story. Hearing everything in our friendship was a lie hurts. I actually truly cared for him, or the him that I thought I knew. When he tells me I was so desperate I didn't question anything, I feel like an idiot. How could I have not seen this evil lurking inside him? Thinking back over our short friendship I realize he is partially right. I never once questioned anything. He never talked about himself. We never went to his place. I've been wondering why he was never caught by Calder. Calder has been watching me for the past few weeks and Michael has been around longer than that. I realize he always used the back entrance and only ever came over at night. They say hindsight is twenty-twenty and, boy, is that true. Every single thing he has said or not said, done or not done now makes sense. I know there's no hope in reasoning with him but I try anyway, "You don't have to do this. Just let me go. I'm sure my father will give you whatever you want."

"Oh, sweetheart," his face turns into a condescending fake sympathetic frown, "It isn't personal. That would require me caring about you at all. What I feel for you is nothing. You are a means to an end and that end is lots and lots of money. Besides, my reputation is worth even more than you. You wouldn't imagine how hard I've had to work to prove myself. And it's paid off and I'm now one of the most sought out hired help."

You would think after everything he's said and everything I've gone through I should be paralyzed by fear. Even right now, I'm strapped to a chair with my arms tied behind my back and I'm most likely going to be meeting my maker pretty soon. But I can't help the sarcastic retort from popping out of my mouth, "Oh, your mother would be so proud."

His demeanor changes and his face narrows. I'm saved by the bell. Or I should say ring since his phones rings right at that moment. He walks away and answers it. I try to listen but I can't hear anything so I try to find something to help me escape. Not that if I find anything it will help since my self-defense and escaping skills haven't magically improved during our conversation. Mabel was right and I should have taken that self-defense class. Regrets aren't going to help me escape. Craning my neck around, I see that the back wall is one big garage like door and one regular door in the corner. No help there. I glance up and see that there's actually a little upstairs area, again, not remotely useful unless I can fly. I let out a breath as any hope I had of escaping deflates.

I glance up when I hear Michael's voice turn harsh and cold. His footsteps pound into the floor as he shoves his phone in my face. "Say something." Looking from the phone to his face, I shake my head. If I can't escape and he's using me to blackmail my dad who can help put away a bad man and save people's lives then I'll have to be strong and brave. He narrows his eyes at me as he says slowly repeats, "Say something." I turn my head away. That's where I make my mistake. With my head turned I don't have any warning to the knife that slashes across my stomach. My breath catches at the sting and then my strangled scream comes once my mind processes the pain. The knife didn't go deep enough to cut through the muscle or anything vital but based on the burn and the pain it is definitely going to need stitches. His smile shows he is proud of himself and that he's enjoying this. I still don't know how I never saw or sensed this side to Michael. He's always been sassy and not very attuned to other people's needs, but the cold calculated look covering his face chills me to the bone. "Want to try this again, sunshine?"

There are tears streaming down my cheeks as he places his phone next to my ear. I can hear my name being called on the other end. The voice sounds frantic. Apparently I took too long to say something because I feel the bite of his knife swipe just above my left knee. All thoughts and hopes of being strong and self sacrificing fly out the window. I'm scared that I'm going to be tortured to death for a man I've never met and never will get the chance to meet. "Help. Help. Please help me. Please." I sob into the phone.

Michael places the phone back up against his ear and walks away again. I'm disappointed that I gave in. Since the beginning of this whole ordeal right up until Michael cut me I've had a handle on this situation. Or at least as much of a handle as anyone could hope to have. But it's all too much. I don't want to be strong and brave anymore and all those heroines are full of crap. Self-preservation is too strong of an instinct to ignore. It dawns on me that just because I had a momentary lapse in my composure doesn't mean I can't still be the strong heroine in my story. If no white knight is going to come rescue me, I'll have to find a way to rescue myself. When he gets off the phone, I take a cue from those books and movies and in a bid to buy some time I tell him I have to go to the bathroom.

His reply is quick and short, "No."

I try to think of another excuse when an idea pops into my

head. I'd already used it as an excuse once today, why not keep with the pattern? Michael's always been disgusted and put off with anything having to do with that time of the month, so I repeat my lie from earlier. "I'm on my period. So unless you want a bloody mess to clean up, and not the type of bloody mess you're used to cleaning up. Let. Me. Use. The. Bathroom."

Looking me up and down his face wrinkles with disgust, "How anyone finds anything to do with the female anatomy attractive is beyond me; it's appalling." Letting out a huff, he continues, "Fine. But if you think this is your big chance to get away, know that I'm smarter than you. There is no way for you to escape from the bathroom." I feel the ropes around my wrists give way and then hear a click and the feel of cool metal replaces the ropes. His hand wraps around my bicep and he yanks me to my feet. I'm shoved in front of him and he pushes me to the bathroom. The empty handcuff is clicked around the sink plumbing. "Ugh, I'm going to be out there. No way am I staying in here. Yell when you're done." He slams the door on his way out.

Reaching my arm as far as I can, I twist and look around. My side burns and I wince at the pain stretching open the wound causes. Only a small sink and an old toilet make up the bathroom. There isn't even a window. I plop on the toilet as

167

despair and hopelessness crashes into me for what feels like the millionth time. The reality of the situation is I'm trapped and there is no hope that I can get out myself. No chance to be the hero of my own story. My only hope is that Calder will find me. Only, I don't even know if Calder is alive. Sobs rack my body as I silently weep. No one is going to find me and no one is going to save me. There doesn't seem much of a point to even fight anymore. My hand automatically goes to my necklace and I panic when it's not there. Frantic I look all around the bathroom and even in my shirt. I must have lost it in the struggle with Michael. My last connection to my mom is lost. Bone numbing despair hits me and I cry. They always say to not let them see you cry. Don't show weakness. I'm numb and no longer care. Dejected, I yell out for him to come and get me.

I'm thrown back into the chair and this time instead of rope my wrists are handcuffed to each other with the metal handcuffs from the bathroom. The rope is now used to secure each of my ankles to one of the legs of the chair. Darkness has washed over the warehouse. All of the overhead lights are either burned out or turned off except for the row right above me. My stomach growls and I realize how hungry I am. Michael must have heard it because he looks at my stomach and then shrugs his shoulders and walks away towards the office. I'm left alone and time seems at a standstill. The only other light is pouring through the office door that Michael left slightly ajar.

I've been staring up at the light for who knows how long. My neck is starting to get stiff and sore, so I try to stretch it out. There is a spider crawling on the floor and the minimal lighting ups the creep factor of its shadow. If I were still the normal old Imogen I would be freaking out, especially when it starts to crawl towards me. But in the grand scheme of things a spider, even a poisonous one, seems like a walk in the park. I must have zoned out watching the spider. My eyes start to water and burn from being held open. I blink them a few times to get the burning feeling to go away. The knife wounds to my side and knee are now a bearable dull throbbing ache. Unable to fight the overwhelming exhaustion anymore, I let my head roll forward and down onto my chest and let sleep take me into its sweet oblivion.

A noise rouses me from the brink of deep sleep. I glance around but don't see anything except the light from the office. My shoulders fall and I exhale the breath I didn't know I had been holding. I'm about to fall asleep again when I get a sense of something behind me. You know when you have that inexplicable feeling that something is watching you? Or

169

when you sense someone's touch right before it happens? That's what I feel. There isn't longer than a half of a second to ponder what it could be when a large strong hand clamps over my mouth. Another large hand wraps around my hands. Goosebumps break out across my body at the feeling of warm breathing at my ear.

"I'm going to move my hand so I can undo the handcuffs. Are you going to be a good girl and not scream?" The sound of Rice's voice in my ear sends a mixture of relief and confusion coursing through me. Tears spring from the corners of my eyes as I nod my head. "Don't say a word or make noise." Even though there is no way my mind could form words right now I figure I need to reassure him so I nod. He removes the hand from my mouth and I feel him working at the cuffs on my wrists. The handcuffs fall away without noise and then I feel the ropes at my ankles follow suit. I turn and see his outstretched hand. I'm still confused as to how and why Rice is even here. My mind starts to reason that this has to be a dream. Since that seems like a logical explanation I put my confusion and doubt to the side. If I can't escape in real life then I'm definitely escaping in my dream. My subconscious handed me a white knight straight out of my fantasies.

I grab his hand and tip toe behind him towards the back

corner of the warehouse where I had seen a door. My whole body is stiff and I'm slow from exhaustion. This is my dream, and my subconscious doesn't even have the gall to let me not feel anything. What kind of crap is this? We're almost to the door when the office door slams against a wall. I feel Rice yank me in front of him and shove me towards the door. A gunshot rings out and the ringing in my ears and the feeling of his hands pushing me jolt me to reality. This isn't a dream and Rice is actually here and he is rescuing me. There isn't a yell or outcry after the gunshot so I'm assuming no one was hit. Rice fires a gun that he seemingly conjured out of thin air and if I was still under the impression that this was indeed a dream he probably would have. Michael cries out and I know he's been hit. I can't help the little ball of anxiety that forms in my stomach at the thought of my friend getting hurt. It's still hard to remember that he isn't my friend and I shouldn't care what happens to him. Another gunshot sounds as we break through the door. Rice yells, "Keep running. Run straight and right for that dark line, those are trees. I'm right behind you! Whatever you do, don't look back."

I hesitate for an instant before I follow his orders. I run faster than I have ever run before. The dark line of the trees gets bigger the closer I get. It's like one tall dark wall. My lungs are on fire as I make it to the thick coverage of trees and bushes. I stop and bend over, trying to catch my breath but Rice is pulling on my arm. "We can't stop. We have to keep moving." He takes the lead and I try to follow him as best as I can. I can feel the warmth of blood trickling down my side and down my leg. My lungs are still burning as I'm stumbling trying to navigate in the dark. Rice must not remember that his legs are like twice the length of mine because he just seems to keep getting farther and farther ahead of me. I'm trying to hurry as fast as I can limp but I keep tripping over tree roots and rocks.

Finally I hiss in a loud whisper, "Stop!" Leaves and twigs snap under his feet as he makes his way back to me. "In case you missed it, I have a gash across my knee and my stomach is basically cut open. I'm exhausted. My lungs are on fire. I can't see where I'm going because unlike you I wasn't blessed with night vision. I keep tripping. Plus your legs are like a million feet longer than mine. I'm done. I'm stopping here." Okay so I'm exaggerating a little. But I'm tired and I'm hungry and my body hurts and I'm thoroughly confused. What is he doing here? In the moonlight dancing through the trees I see him pinch the bridge of his nose in agitation. He drops his hand to his side and squeezes his hands into fists a couple times then comes over to me and hoists me up on his shoulder. I was wrong thinking he didn't know about my cuts because as he settles me on his shoulder he is mindful to make it my good side. A squeak escapes me before my protests start, "Put me down! Rice, you put me down this instant! You can't do this. We're not cave people."

"If you aren't going to walk then I'm going to have to carry you. I can't leave you here or you'll get yourself killed and I don't want that. Now stop moving and be quiet."

"Oh, I don't care what you want, mister! I have been kidnapped, cut, sleep deprived, and I am starving. I am not going to add man-handled to the list! You. Put. Me. Down!" I start hitting him with my hands and attempting to kick him with my feet. The sting of his hand hitting across my butt shocks me into stopping.

I can hear the smile on his voice as he says, "Good girl." Then he continues into the forest. You would think that my added weight would have slowed him down but he seems to be handling it like I weigh little more than a feather. While I still have a million questions running through my mind about who he is, why he is here, how he is here, the feel of his arm across the back of my thighs and my view of his glorious backside does a lot to settle me down. Don't get me wrong, I'm going to be grilling him the second he puts me down but right now he is adding distance between me and a crazy person and I am taking advantage of that.

After what feels like twenty miles but I'm assured wasn't even two he stops and sets me down. He bends forward and backwards stretching out his back and I'm happy to see that he was affected by carrying me since he was such a jerk about it. Now that we seem to be relatively safe and the fear and despair I was feeling before is gone, I take a good long look at him. I know he is wearing a leather jacket because I could feel the soft smoothness as he was carrying me. Looking at him now I see he has brought an arsenal with him. He is wearing one of those gun holsters that go on like a backpack with a gun on each side of his ribs. There is a huge scary looking Rambo knife attached at his hip and another gun on the other hip.

"So who are you? Or I guess maybe I should say, what are you? You obviously aren't a coffee roaster." I should be more scared or nervous. But with all the unknowns and unanswered questions, I know without a doubt that Rice isn't here to hurt me.

He starts pacing and I can tell he is having a conversation

174

with himself in his head, "Well, actually, um, your dad kind of sort of sent me." Afraid of my reaction he seems to brace himself for whatever I'm about to unleash.

Although I knew he had to be more than just a guy who roasts and sells coffee - I mean he looks like he could give Jason Bourne a run for his money - him being sent by my dad and being mafia never crossed my mind. I stand there trying to process everything. I turn to him and throw my hand up, "Are you *kidding* me?! Is anyone in my life who they say they are? Is June a ninja? Mabel is Interpol?" The reality of the situation and the fact that so many people I thought I knew and could trust are actually big fat lying liars hits me. My knees go weak and I plop myself down on the dirt. "How? I've known you for, like, what, five or six months? I thought my dad didn't know about me until like four months ago?"

"Actually he's known about you for almost a year. He was hoping by keeping his distance he could keep you safe. But about six months ago he had a falling out with Manuel. Your dad wanted to cut ties but Manuel didn't want that. Afraid that Manuel would find out about you, which in the end he did, he wanted someone to be close enough to keep you safe. So he sent me down here."

"Wow. What am I supposed to say to that? I get trying to keep me safe but why wouldn't he reach out to me? Didn't he want to know me? Doesn't he care about me?" For the first time in my whole life I am overcome with the feeling of being unwanted. My dad has known about me for a year but hasn't done anything about it. The tears start to fall as I wish desperately that my mom was alive and here to hold me through the pain. Rice rushes over and cradles me in his arm.

"The moment he found out about you he wanted to fly down here and get you. But everything he's been working years for was about to happen. And when that did, the threat and risk to you would have been too much. So he kept tabs on you and watched you. When it was safe he was going to reach out. But then Manuel put a hit on you and he had no choice to go to the police once our resources were exhausted."

His words offer me a little comfort but I still feel unwanted. Like an inconvenience you have to deal with. "So who are you? I mean like in the operation, who are you?"

He notices as I shiver so he removes his jacket and puts it around my shoulders. Then he wraps his arm around my back and pulls me into him and leans back against a tree. "Well, that's going to be a long story."

"Seeing as I have so many places to go," I trail off.

"Fair enough. My dad was friends with your dad actually. They were best friends growing up and when your dad took over the family business my dad was right there next to him as his right hand man." He rubs his hand up and down my arm as he continues, "My parents were high school sweethearts. They got married after graduation. I was born six years later. My sister came four years after me. A year after that, your dad married Theresa and they got pregnant with Marie. Your grandfather was starting to groom your father to take over the family business and wanted him to settle down." The excitement I feel at finding out I have a sister is weighed down with jealousy that she grew up with the dad I didn't.

Unaware of my conflicting emotions he continues, "My youngest sister followed about two years later. My father was killed doing business six months after my youngest sister was born. I was seven. Your dad took it as his responsibility to make sure that we were taken care of. Since Theresa and your dad couldn't have any more children after Marie, I was sort of like the son your dad never had and he was the father figure I needed. Theresa was like a second mother to me. Your dad's been trying to build up legitimate businesses so that he can get out of all of the illegal business dealings. He has been grooming me to take over the business and didn't want to leave it to me wrapped up in illegal activity. It's always been my fate that I'll run things when your dad retires."

"Why would he want to do that? Isn't that the opposite of what the mafia is?"

"There was an accident about ten years ago. Marie was out for prom. She'd begged your dad to let her go since she wasn't quite sixteen yet. Your dad was wrapped around her finger. Well, he finally agreed but only if our guys could drive them. Someone ran them off the road on the way home from the dance. Our guys were killed. Her date lived but is paralyzed from the waist down." My heart drops when I think that she didn't make it. I'm disgusted that I felt any negative feelings towards someone who lost their life so young. "She fared a little better. Her right arm was crushed and she lost it from the elbow down. She also broke her leg and ankle. But she lived. She walks with a limp but she never lets her disadvantages affect her life."

"So she is alive?! My sister is alive?"

"Yes, yes, she's very much alive." I let out the breath I was holding. "She is in school to be a teacher. It took a lot of her begging to finally convince your dad. He's overly protective of anyone he considers family but he takes it to another level with her. Kids love her and she's going to be a great teacher. She doesn't take crap from anyone. She thinks she is bigger and tougher than she is and I can't tell you how many times I've had to save her." The emotion in his voice tells me he cares a great deal for her. Jealousy rears its ugly head again when I think of them having a romantic relationship. I have no claim on Rice but the thought of another woman being with him makes me see red. All we have shared is a kiss and some flirting and casual touching. It isn't his fault that I read more into his actions.

Trying to change the subject I ask, "What about Mezzanote? Is that all a cover and lie too?"

"Actually, no." I can hear the smile and how proud he is on his voice. "That was all my idea. When he found out about you and your café he started to worry about you and how he could keep an eye on things from so far away. That gave me the idea of becoming a supplier. He was looking for more business ventures and coffee is a profitable one. So he bought a coffee bean farm in Mexico and then the rest is history. Since it was my idea he sort of handed the reins and let me do what I wanted. I found someone who was knowledgeable in coffee roasting and we came up with our own blends and it's sort of taken off."

"Wow. Well I'm glad at least some of it wasn't a lie," I manage to say through a yawn.

"Try to get some sleep. We'll need to head out as early as we can. In the dark I can't be exactly sure where we are. I'll have to figure out how far off course we are in the morning."

I lay my head on his chest and nod. His steady breathing and the beat of his heart lull me off to sleep.

- Rice -

I feel her breath even out and her body relax against mine. Thinking back on the last couple of hours, my arm tightens around her. When I saw him take her at the grocery store I was out of my car racing down the street before I even knew what I was doing. He had her in the trunk and was driving away before I even made it to the grocery store. I hopped back in my car and followed them until he turned down a dirt road. I parked and followed them the rest of the way on foot.

After looking around and assessing the location, I went back to the car and went to get my guns. That'll be something I will regret for the rest of my life. I should have followed after them and gotten her out. Thinking about what that maniac put her through, I grind my teeth together in anger. When I get my hands on him, he is going to pay for what he did to her. My slug to his thigh will have to do until I can wrap my hands around his neck.

Thinking of the attitude and fire in her eyes when she was arguing with me makes me chuckle. She has to be one of the only women I know who would be tossing around attitude after what she went through. I love that she says what she thinks and she doesn't put up with any crap. Not seeing her and being able to be the one to protect her for the last few days has been killing me. I didn't realize how much I look forward to seeing her all the time.

I remember when I first saw her picture when John found out about her. She was gorgeous. But that was it, intense attraction. That was all it could be. John is very protective of his family and the way to protect her was to keep her out of our lifestyle until it was safe. But that was where John was in denial; our lifestyle is never going to be safe. He has too many contacts and knows too much. I saw that and he didn't. It's why I've always tried to keep her an arm's length away. Sure there have been a few times where I've slipped and that kiss the other day, it almost did me in. But I stopped myself before things went too far.

It started to change when he sent me down here to watch out for her. I'll never forget when he called me into his office and explained how serious the threat was on her. He didn't trust anyone to come and keep her safe but me. How to do I repay him for everything he's done for me? Getting to close to the daughter he sent me to protect. The one thing he asked me to do was to keep her safe and out of anything remotely connected to our world. When I first walked into her café to try to sell her our coffee, I was blown away by her natural beauty. Her pictures didn't even do her justice.

Once I started doing deliveries, I got to know how amazing she is. Like how she would run out into the middle of traffic to try and save an animal in the middle of the street. She will drop everything if someone she cares about needs her. She's resilient. After everything she has been through, she is still optimistic and sees the best in the world. I laugh and smile more when I am with her than when I am with anyone else. Not everyone gets her sarcasm and humor.

Stopping that kiss the hardest thing I have ever done in my life. I wanted nothing more than to keep kissing her but I would never disrespect John like that. No, he would have to approve before anything could happen between us. So I pulled away and in return caused her to run away. That was the last time I saw her before everything blew up our faces.

I'm content to just hold her right now. The feel of her in my arms is constant reassurance that she's actually here and safe. Here in the dark it's easy to trick myself into thinking things are okay and everything is back to normal. I'm not getting any sleep tonight because I know it's not safe out here in the dark and I have to be on alert. Nothing and no one is going to hurt her again. The next few hours are spent trying to figure out where we are. The ground is damp and the air is muggy. There was a river running behind the warehouse and my guess is we are fairly close to it. I'll be able to get my bearings more in the morning.

CHAPTER ELEVEN

- Rice -

When everything starts to turn to the muted gray of dawn I gently lay her down to look around. I glance back at her curled up body on the ground and there's a small pang in my chest. I don't think I'll ever forgive myself for not being able to keep her from getting hurt. Walking out and through the trees, I realize we are a lot closer to the river than I thought. It is less than fifty yards to the east of us going by the sunrise. We can follow this down to a road and then we can find our way out. I check around us in the other directions and then check to make sure Imogen is still asleep. I head back to the river in the hopes I can find something to use to catch some food. Since I know she hasn't eaten in almost twenty-four hours and I also know how she is when is hungry, I don't want to risk not having something for her when she wakes up.

Luckily John taught me a lot of things growing up that I didn't think I would ever need. I'm not saying he is one of those crazy preppers but he definitely saw the benefit in having unique skills. Right now I am thanking him. I used to argue and hate every second of my survival and military training. If he hadn't made me do that training then I wouldn't have known what to do with the old beer can I just found. I snap the tab off the top and I'll use the can later. Setting the tab on the flattest rock I can find I take my knife and at an angle, I cut an opening in the bottom hole. After a few minutes of sharpening and shaping the hook it's done. I take off the thin band of paracord I wear around my wrist. It was something John insisted on during training. Now it's just a habit, most of the time I forget I'm wearing it. Cutting it open I start to pull the inner strands out. Once I have what looks like enough length I cut it and shove what's left of everything else in my pocket. Once I get the hook tied and the rope tied to a stick I dig around in the ground until I find a worm.

I have to toss out the line a couple times before I get a bite. The first bite I get ends up being too small. I throw out a few more times until I get another bite. This one is still a little small but it'll have to do. Trying my luck one more I time I find another worm and toss it out. I'm just about to call it when I get one. This fella's big and he makes me work for it but eventually I wear him down. My knife isn't the most ideal fish cleaning knife so they come out a little mangled but food is food.

Then I take the can and fill it up with some water from the river. It should be relatively clean after we boil it. It's not ideal but I know she hasn't had much to drink in the last twenty four hours and we have a pretty good walk ahead of us. I'm not sure how long either of us will last in the heat and humidity if we don't get at least some water in.

I go back to where I left Imogen. Judging by the light, I'm guessing I've been gone for a couple hours. When I get to her, she's awake and leaning against the tree with my jacket around her. She stands when she sees me. She looks relieved for a brief second before it turns into anger. Limping over to me she slaps me across the face. "How dare you leave me all alone. I woke up and you were gone. Have you ever been scared out of your mind in a forest all by yourself? No? Well, let me tell you, every single little noise was Michael coming to finish what he started. Then I was afraid he had dragged you off and murdered you. Then he was going to come back for me. But that wasn't believable because there is no way Michael could have dragged you anywhere and it would have been easier for him to just take me. So then I figured you decided to just leave me here to fend for myself." She's rambling. She does that when she gets worked up or nervous.

"Are you done?" I see when she notices the fish because her eyes widen.

"Are you kidding me? You caught some fish? What did you catch them with, your bare hands?" she asks incredulously.

"Actually with a beer can tab."

"Seriously? You're like freaking MacGyver. What are you going to do next? Make a fire with some gum, a paperclip, and a stick?"

I bark out a laugh, "That would be something wouldn't it? No, I have flint on my keychain for that. I'm just going to go and get some kindling from a dead tree I saw on my way back. Everything around here's too wet to start a fire." When I get to the dead tree I cut out some bark to get to the fibers inside. After digging and cutting out what I need, I gather it together and cut a strip from the bottom of my shirt and tie it to a stick I found. I grab my flint rod from my keychain. I scrape some magnesium onto the kindling and then turn the rod and flip my knife over. It takes a couple strikes but it finally lights. I set my keys down and cup my hands around the small flame and breathe some air into it. Slowly and carefully I make my way back to her.

Once I get the fire going I put a stick through the fish's mouths and put them over the fire. I set the can next to the fire so the water can boil. Imogen is silently watching me, when I'm done I go sit next to her.

"So," she says as she bumps her knee against mine.

I nudge her back as I respond, "So."

"I guess I never really thanked you for rescuing me. So, thanks for that. And I guess I should probably say sorry for slapping you."

Smiling I say, "You're welcome and I probably deserved it." We sit in companionable silence just watching the small flames of the fire for a few minutes. I check on the fish and rotate them before I sit back down.

"So what do we do now? I'll need to find a way to get in contact with the FBI. Oh and Calder." Her face falls and her breath catches. If her voice hadn't revealed her emotion then the tears filling her eyes would have. I know she has feelings for him. This realization hits me like a ton of bricks. "I don't even know what happened to him. I don't even know if he's alive!"

I wrap my arm around her and try to console her. "We'll get out of here. And when we do we'll find out about him, I promise." Even though it rips me apart to say it, I mean it. I can tell that he means something to her and I would do anything to help put her fears at ease. Out of fear and anxiety she pulls her bottom lip through her teeth. I'm having a hard time keeping myself from stopping it with my lips. That's the last thing she needs right now. I meet her eyes and she nods her head and then wipes her eyes. Not trusting myself to keep my self-control, I go and check on the fish. They're done so I pull them off. I move the water away from the fire so it can start cooling down as we eat. I pull the skin off the fish and then carefully pull out the backbone and hand it to her. "Make sure to watch out for bones."

"Thank you," she says before she takes a bite. Her eyes close and she lets out a moan, "This is the best thing I have ever tasted."

Her moans send my mind to other ways to make her moan like that. I shake that thought away, "Then you haven't had my waffles." She glances up at me through her eyelashes and

I'm awarded one of her huge beaming smiles.

"I love waffles. You'll have to make them for me sometime." She looks a little embarrassed at her request. Changing the subject her face turns a little more serious as she says, "Seriously, thank you. Thank you for everything." After that we eat in companionable silence.

Once we're done I help her up and then grab the can of water. Rather than carry it while we walk we each drink then start making our way following the river. From what I remember from the little bit of scouting I did, there should be a dirt road a few miles from here. Or at least where I think here is. We move along slowly. Her body is stiff and sore from everything that has happened. Sleeping on the ground last night probably didn't help. But she's a trooper. She hasn't complained once. If I didn't think she'd hit me again, I'd offer to carry her.

"Ever heard of twenty questions," she asks.

"Yeah, of course I have."

"Okay, then what's your most embarrassing moment?"

"You just go right for the good stuff don't you? I'll have to remember that when it's my turn to ask a question."

"Don't answer that one! I want to change my question."

"Nope, it's too late for that. There are no take backs in twenty questions." I hurry so she can't argue, "My most embarrassing moment. Hmmm. Well it would probably have to be when I was twelve. I dove into the public pool and lost my swim trunks. I had to swim around trying to find them. When I finally found them they had sunk to the bottom of the pool. As I dove down to try and get them the lifeguard thought I was drowning and dove in and pulled me out. Only I hadn't had a chance to grab my shorts so she pulled me out completely naked. To make matters worse she was the hot lifeguard all of us drooled over. Now it's my turn. Time for a doozy." I pause after every word, "What, is, your, absolute, worst, pet peeve?"

She lets out a laugh as she answers, "Seriously? That's all you are going to hit me with?"

"Hey lady, I have nineteen more questions. Just hold your horses. I'll get to the good ones later."

"Okay, if you say so." She pauses like she is thinking. "I would have to say that my worst pet peeve is when people have messy eyebrows."

191

We're still hiking through the trees and she is a little ways behind me, so I glance back and raise my eyebrow at her. "Messy eyebrows huh? Interesting. So if I, let's say, did this," I take my finger and go along my eyebrow in the opposite direction, "It would totally freak you out."

"Yes, so don't be an ass. Fix it. Please."

"Yes dear." I fix my eyebrow and start walking again once she catches up to me.

"My turn again. What is your favorite candy?"

"That's easy, it's bubble gum."

"That isn't a candy, that's gum."

"Hey, these are my answers. If I want to say gum is my favorite candy I can if I want to," I tease.

"Why bubble gum?"

"Nuh uh, it's my turn to ask a question."

I can hear the eye roll when she responds, "Fine. It's your turn."

"If you were a dinosaur, what dinosaur would you be?"

"What?"

"It's a serious question. You can tell a lot from a person by the type of dinosaur they want to be."

"Considering I've never thought about what dinosaur I would be, let me think for a second." She takes about a minute before she answers, "I would be Ducky, from the Land Before Time. Or whatever type of dinosaur she is, I don't the scientific name."

"Interesting."

"So what does that say about me?"

"Is that your next question?"

"Grrr." She actually growls at me. "I never figured you would be such a stickler for the rules. No, that is *not* my next question. Why bubble gum?"

"It reminds me of my dad. Since I was only seven when he died I don't have a lot of memories of him. Most of what I can remember revolved around baseball. He loved the Red Sox. My mom told him she would leave him if he kept chewing so he switched to bubble gum. Just the smell can make me think of him. I guess I just kept up the habit."

I don't think she was expecting a sentimental reason

because she doesn't say anything for a while. When she finally does all she says is, "Your turn."

We continue asking each other questions for the next little bit. Some are more serious and deep and others are superficial and fun. We finally make it to a dirt road. It's taken a couple hours to get here and now glancing up and down, I can see that we have another good walk before we find a car. Turning and looking at her, I'm not sure she'll be able to keep walking.

"We probably have another half mile or so before we find a car. Do you think you are going to be able to make it? Should we take a break?"

She winces as she bends over to catch her breath, "No. No I don't want to be here anymore. I want a shower. I want food. I want water. And mostly I want, no, I *need* chocolate. If you promise me chocolate, I will walk wherever you want me to."

"That's my girl," I say with pride. The late afternoon sun is beating down us. We've been walking along this road for over an hour and I haven't seen one car go by. I'm starting to worry that we need to find water when we come across some cars. It looks like they parked in front of an older dock of some sort. I hold my hand up to signal Imogen to stop. I whisper to her, "You stay here. I'll signal for you to follow me." She silently nods her head.

I quietly sneak up to the first car and check the handle. Someone is smiling down on us because the door is unlocked. Even better is it's an older model without an alarm. Glancing back to Imogen I motion for her to come to where I am. When she gets to me I tell her to get in the back and I get in the front. I check for keys in the sun visor and under the seat. I find them in the console in between the seats. I wonder when our luck is going to run out. It never ceases to amaze me how many people leave their keys in the car. After I start the car we pull out and take off.

- Imogen -

It's late afternoon when we finally make it out of the woodsy swamp and find a car. Normally, I would have some qualms about stealing a car but desperate times call for desperate measures. I turn my head to the side and I'm surprised when a wave of exhaustion sweeps over me. My eyes close and I'm asleep before I even know it.

The stopping of the car wakes me up. I glance around and notice the sky is awash with the pinkish glow of the approaching sunset. Glancing at the clock on the dashboard, I realize I've been asleep for a little over an hour. "Sorry I fell asleep. You should have woken me up."

"No, I wanted to let you sleep. You needed it."

He's pulled the car over on a street I don't recognize. Looking over his shoulder, he tells me, "Stay here. I'll be right back."

I'm not given much of a choice as he is out of the door and bounding down the street before I can even respond. Twisting around in my seat I notice that the street looks to be full of apartments and row houses. Rice is back and opening my door.

"Follow me and stay right at my back. If I'm going too fast, tell me." He leads me down the street and then turns left down an alleyway. We cut down another street and then another alleyway. Finally he leads me to a back door of what looks like a row house that has been turned into a couple different apartments or condos. He takes something out of his pocket and jiggles with the lock for a minute and then I'm being lead inside and up the stairs. We approach a door and he does his jiggle thing again and then pulls me inside.

Flicking on the lights, I see we are inside a nice but fairly bare apartment. It's filled with just the basics. Glancing down at the entry table I see a few pieces of mail. I'm not sure what triggers it or why but I just sort of lose it. "Are you kidding me? We can't stay here. I've never even had a ticket and in the span of less than twenty-four hours we've committed grand larceny and now we are going to add breaking and entering onto the list too? And what about," I look back down at the mail to see the name of the person whose house we are breaking into, "Maurice Fitzpatrick? Poor Maurice is going to come home and find out his apartment has been burglarized. Then he is going to call the police. Then they'll come and dust for finger prints and then I'll go to jail. And what if we're still here?" My face falls at my realization, "Oh no. Oh gosh, you're going to have to kill him right? He knows too much. Even if we aren't still here you can't risk him calling the police. So you're going to kill poor old Maurice. He's probably some little old feeble man. But that's what you guys do, right? Whack people who know too much or get in the way? You aren't going to cement his feet and throw him in a river or something or chop him up into little bits?" I start to feel woozy at the thought of this poor man being killed because of me. I didn't even notice that my voice was increasing in volume and octaves. The panic is evident in my voice, "Hurry, we haven't really touched anything we can leave and go somewhere else. We can go back to my place."

I realize I've been wringing my hands together and I've been looking at my feet so I glance up and look at Rice. He is looking at the ceiling and shaking his head. What's even worse is that his shoulders are shaking and I realize he's laughing. And he's laughing at me. I get defensive then. "I'm sorry. But I don't find this funny! Sorry I have more regard for life than you do. Sorry I think it's a big deal to murder someone just because they are an inconvenience, especially after *we* break into *their* house. I can't be here. I can't be here with you. I think…" He grabs me before I can finish my thought.

Putting his hand under my chin and bringing my eyes up to meet his, he says, "Imogen, calm down. We aren't going to kill Maurice."

"We aren't?"

"Well, no. I don't really think that would be helpful," he chuckles again as he continues, "Mostly because I'm Maurice. And we aren't breaking and entering because this is my apartment."

Confusion wrinkles my brow, "But your name is Rice. You picked the locks."

"I set my keys down back by the river and I forgot to pick them up. I didn't even realize until the drive back here. I go by Rice but my name full name is Maurice."

"Rice is short for Maurice? That's the best you could come up with? Why not something like, I don't know off the top my head, Mo?"

"It was my grandfather's name but growing up in Boston, Maurice wasn't really a name you went by if you didn't want to get beat up. Mo probably would have been better. I get some strange looks when people hear Rice. But I didn't pick it. The nickname came from elementary school when something was covering the M-A-U and Pete, my best friend, thought my name was Rice. He made fun of me, I punched him, and we've been best friends ever since. It's just sort of stuck. Now that we've established that I am in fact Maurice and we aren't breaking any more laws, let's get those cuts looked at." He leads me into the bathroom and leaves to grab some first aid supplies. When he comes back in he tells me, "I didn't plan on needing an arsenal of first aid items so I grabbed what I could. All right, let's see them." He looks at me expectantly and I realize he's expecting me to take my pants off so he can see the one on my knee.

"Um, excuse me? I'm not just going to strip my clothes off."

"Imogen, we've been climbing through the swamp. You're dirty and sweaty. I need to clean those cuts and see how deep they really are. What you actually need is the hospital but we can't go there yet so I'm going to need to clean and dress them here." He smiles as he adds, "If it helps, I promise I won't look."

"Har har. Fine." I know he has a point so I grudgingly wiggle my pants off. They get a little stuck on some dried blood on my knee and my breath catches as I tug them past it. He's sitting on the edge of the bathtub so I step in front of him. I feel his hand on the back of my thigh as he lifts my leg and rests my foot on the side of the tub in between his legs.

"This is going to hurt," he warns. Wetting a washcloth in the tub spout, he gently tries to rub along the cut and clean it. My sudden intake of breath stills his movement. He glances up at me, "Are you going to be okay if I keep going?" I nod my head and blink a few tears out of my eyes. Turning my head towards the ceiling I try to breathe through the pain. "Where is the other one?" I pull up the right side of my shirt and I hear him exhale and say something under his breath. The pain I felt when he was cleaning the cut above my knee was nothing compared to the pain of him washing the one on my stomach. His hand resting along my back, bracing me while he cleans, does a little to help distract me but not enough.

"Now this part is gonna hurt like hell," he says. When the alcohol hits the first cut it takes my breath away. I've started doing the labor breathing you see in the movies, the quick shallow fast breaths. As I squeeze my eyelids shut, tears spring from the corners.

He moves up to the cut on my stomach again and on every breath I mutter, "Ouch ouch ouch ouch ouch." Suddenly the pain and the emotions from the last week are all too much and I break down. I feel like I'm on an emotional rollercoaster. One second I'm angry and fighting and then I'm scared and then the next second sobs wrack my body. I'm engulfed in strong steady arms as I'm nestled onto his lap. His hand trails up and down my body and I rest my head on his shoulder as I let the reality of everything finally hit me. I've lost one of my best friends, or at least someone I thought was my best friend. Just because it was all a lie to him doesn't mean it was to mean. My emotions are real and I need to mourn the loss of the friendship I thought it was. I've also been shot at, kidnapped, cut, and lied to. I soak his shirt for a good fifteen minutes. As the sobs subside, I'm suddenly very aware that I am half naked in Rice's arms. My hands grasp his shirt as my head lifts to the crook of his neck. I know he's feeling what I'm feeling because instead of the comforting grip from a few seconds ago, his fingers are now digging into my thigh and shoulder like he is afraid I am going to disappear.

My name is a whisper on his breath, "Imogen." We look into each other's eyes before our lips crash together and our tongues tangle. This kiss isn't sweet or romantic, it's carnal. Full of passion and a myriad of emotions. My hand runs up his neck and tangles in his hair, pulling him even further into me. I feel his hand on my neck as his other hand snakes around my waist pulling my whole body closer to his. As he pulls me into him my side stings and I wince. Hoping it went unnoticed, I try to continue our kiss. I was kidding myself thinking anything would get past him. Bracing myself for another humiliating rejection, I'm surprised when one doesn't come. This time he slows the pace and intensity of the kiss before he gently pulls me away from him.

He stands with me in his arms and tenderly sets me on my feet. Then he reaches into the shower and turns the water on. "I don't want you to do anything you are going to regret. You've also been through a lot and I don't want to take advantage of you. Plus, you need to shower because you smell like swamp. Your muscles will appreciate soaking in the hot water. I probably should have let you do that before cleaning your cuts. I'll grab you some clothes you can put on when you're done. I'll toss your clothes in the washer. If you need anything, call me." Then he presses a kiss to my forehead and leaves.

I'm left standing there reeling from that kiss. Kissing Rice the first time was unlike anything I've ever experienced before. Kissing Rice for the second time was mind blowing. I can only imagine what it would be like if things went further. My hands wrap around me in an effort to keep myself from falling into a million pieces, my side twinges in pain and I'm reminded that I'm really in no condition, emotionally or physically, to enjoy everything that a night with Rice would offer.

Reluctantly I step into the warm spray of the water. I let it warm and massage my tight sore muscles. Grabbing some soap I wash my body, taking care when I get to my cuts. The door opens and I hear Rice call, "Here are some clothes." Then I hear the door click shut again. I shampoo my hair and wince when I feel a big lump and dried blood from where Michael knocked me out. I stand and let the water run down my body until it's no longer warm.

Wrapping myself in a towel, I pick up the clothes Rice left me. There is a pair of soft sweat pants and a large sweatshirt.

I'm looking for a bra and a pair of underwear. Hello, earth to Imogen. Why would he have a bra and underwear? I see he's also left some gauze and bandages. I bandage my cuts and then I pull the sweatshirt over my head. It smells like Rice and I relish the fact that I'm by myself so I can stick my nose in the fabric and try to commit it to memory. When I've gotten my fill of the sweatshirt smell, I glance in the mirror. I look about as good as I feel which isn't saying much. Taking the elastic I've had on my wrist through the whole ordeal, I throw my hair up in a mess on the top of my head.

I open the door and I'm knocked backwards by what I can only describe as a bear. The cutest pair of brown eyes are looking up at me. Footsteps pound as Rice rushes in.

"Bernie! Bernie, leave her alone." He is pulling at the fluffy giant's collar.

A smile breaks out on my face as I stoop down and nuzzle his soft face. "Hi, Bernie." I catch Rice's eyes as I say, "I didn't know you had a dog. He is gorgeous! What breed is he?"

"He's a rescue so I'm not really sure. They told me a St. Bernard mix and that he probably has some Mastiff in him. I think he's part goat since he tries to eat everything. But goat or no goat we're buds and I can't imagine life without him."

He gets a little embarrassed at his confession so I reassure him with another smile.

"I love him. I'm the same way with Mr. Darcy." When his name leaves my mouth my face falls. "Mr. Darcy! I have to get him. He and Cleo are still at Calder's cabin. They're probably freaking out."

"We'll get them tomorrow, I promise. Right now you need to have some more food and you need to drink something. We'll get a good night's rest tonight and then we will head out early in the morning and get them. They'll be okay until tomorrow morning."

I don't like it but I know that I don't have much of a choice. When it comes to Rice I've learned that it's usually what he says goes. He raises his eyebrow almost wanting me to try and fight him. Raising my hands in surrender I say, "Okay, fine. But first thing in the morning we are going to get them."

"Promise. Dinner's almost ready," he turns and heads to the kitchen. I follow him with Bernie right by my side. As we enter I can hear music playing softly. I recognize the song almost immediately.

"Hozier? You know Hozier?"

"Good guess. Yeah, I love his voice. I've wanted to go to one of his concerts but things keep coming up." I have a feeling I'm one of those things if not all of them. There is a living room connected to the kitchen and Bernie goes and hops up on the couch. Not wanting to abandon Rice, I stay standing in the kitchen.

"So, what's for dinner?"

"Well, since my fish was such a hit, I decided to make you my famous waffles."

"I was joking about you making them for me. But I'm starving and they sound so good. Keep cooking like this for me and you might never get rid of me."

He's barely audible but I think I hear him say, "That's the plan." Then again it could be my overactive imagination at work. It wouldn't be the first time. The smells coming from where he is are making my mouth water. Looking back at me he motions to the couch with his chin, "Go relax. I'm fine in here. I'll bring it to you when I'm done."

I go and sit next to Bernie who moves over so his head is resting on my leg. Petting him is soothing and comforting. Sitting here, I lay my head back and listen to the music. I never knew Rice and I had such similar tastes in music. Although I'm not sure I'm going to be hearing Jay Z or Wicked anytime soon. So far I've heard quite a few bands I recognize. Most of the people I know have never heard of most of these people so for him to have them all on a playlist is intriguing.

Rice gently touches my elbow and hands me a plate. I must have dozed off. "Thank you. This smells amazing."

He sits next to me on the couch. There isn't much small talk going on. I would probably eat anything I'm so hungry, but this tastes even better than it smells. The waffles are swimming in syrup and there are strawberries sprinkled on top. Everything is topped off with whipped cream. I'm shoveling waffle into my mouth and the only thing I'm doing in between bites is taking a breath. After my very realistic impression of a Hoover vacuum I sit back and let the food settle. He glances at me as I stretch out and starts laughing.

"You inhaled that. I'm not sure I've seen anyone eat that much food that fast."

"You don't want to get between me and food," I joke.

"Noted. Now that you're done, if you're tired you can head

to bed if you want. I'm giving you my bed and I'm taking the couch. I'll try to keep Bernie out here but he is sneaky when he wants to be and he'll probably find his way in and up on the bed in the middle of the night."

"Oh you don't have to give me your bed. I'm more than fine on the couch, really. But I'm actually surprisingly not that tired right now. Do you want to watch a movie or something?"

"You're taking my bed and that's the end of it. I'll carry you in there and lock the door. If my mom found out I let a woman sleep on the couch while I was on the bed I would never hear the end of it. Plus your dad would probably kill me," he shudders at the thought. Continuing he says, "I'm game for a movie or whatever. I don't have much here since this place is only temporary. I have a few basic cable channels." He flips through the channels he has but there isn't much on. His movie selection is even sadder. There is a *Friends* marathon on one of the channels so we decide on that. You can't go wrong with *Friends*.

I glance over at Rice after the sixth episode and see that he has fallen asleep. Like a creeper I watch him sleep for a few minutes. I know he would be more comfortable if I go in the bedroom so he can have the whole couch but I can't bring myself to leave him. I move my legs and scoot closer to him. I only make it a few more episodes before I too fall asleep.

CHAPTER TWELVE

- Imogen -

I wake up nestled into Rice's side with his arm around me. Afraid that if I open my eyes it'll end, I continue to lie here with my eyes shut. I feel him chuckle and then he says, "I know you're awake. You can open your eyes now."

Sheepishly I open my eyes to see him looking down at me. Cue the embarrassing tomato face blushing. He smiles at my discomfort before saying, "Good morning."

"Good morning."

"So I was thinking we could eat a quick breakfast and then head out. We'll need to stop by the shop before we head to get Mr. Darcy." At the hopeful look on my face he adds, "And by shop I mean mine not yours. It isn't safe to go to yours yet."

Swallowing my disappointment I acquiesce, "OK."

We both stand and head into the kitchen. Rice gets some coffee started and then turns to me, "Your clothes are dry. I put them on the bed last night after you fell asleep out here. I was going to move you but I was afraid I would wake you up and I figured you needed your sleep."

My heart lifts when I learn that it wasn't my sneaky moves after he fell asleep that caused our cuddling this morning, but it was his choice. He came back to the couch even after he had woken up and I was sleeping. "I don't think I realized how exhausted I was. I'm going to go change so we can go get Mr. Darcy and Cleo."

He turns back towards the kitchen and I head to his bedroom. I thought the sweatshirt smelled amazing but it doesn't hold a candle to the smell of Rice's bedroom. Imagining him lying in the bed makes my stomach do a little flip. I spot my clothes on his bed. Even though they've been cleaned they're still stained with blood and dirt. Since I don't have anything else and I pull them on and head back out to Rice.

There is cereal and milk on the counter. Rice is sitting, drinking a cup of coffee with an empty bowl in front of him. He's absent-mindedly stroking Bernie's head. When Bernie sees me he gets up and runs over. I give him a good scratch behind his ears and then we both head over to where Rice is sitting.

"Hey," he says when I sit next to him.

"Hey."

"There is some cereal and coffee. If that doesn't sound good feel free to look through the cabinets, you're welcome to whatever you want. I'm going to go change," he says as he stands. To Bernie he adds, "Come on, Bern."

However Bernie doesn't budge. Reaching down and petting his head again, I say, "He's fine here."

He turns to head to his room and under his breath he mutters, "Traitor. Give me up for a pretty girl."

I look down at Bernie and he looks up at me and I shrug my shoulders. Not one to miss an opportunity to get to know Rice just a little bit better, I get up and start looking through his cabinets. There really isn't anything in them; it's really just the bare necessities. I laugh when I get to a cabinet that has a value size bucket full of Double Bubble. Since I'm not going to learn much else from snooping through cabinets I give up and pour myself a cup of coffee.

I look at the cereals he has out on the counter and I laugh inwardly at his selection. Rice comes off as confident almost to the point of cockiness. He is strong and hard and not someone you would want to pick a fight with. But he also has a soft side and he makes me laugh. I'm now realizing he also has the tastes of a little kid. Three cereals are on the counter and they are all chock full of sugar with brightly colored boxes. My choices are Cinnamon Toast Crunch, Fruit Loops, or Reese's Peanut Butter Puffs.

I settle on the Reese's, my rationale being that since there has to be some peanut butter in there somewhere at least I'm getting some protein. Plus I have Cinnamon Toast Crunch and Fruit Loops at home. Bernie's soulful brown eyes are watching me optimistically. His bowl is sitting against the wall so I grab the Fruit Loops and pour a few in his bowl. Patting his head, I coo, "Good boy."

He devours his cereal in four bites. I'm not quite as Hoover vacuum like today so I've still got about a quarter of my cereal left when Rice walks back in. I hurry and finish and then walk to the sink and clean my bowl. "I'm ready."

"Let's do this," he enthuses. He hooks Bernie's leash on and explains unnecessarily, "He normally comes to the shop with me. I feel bad leaving him again after I've been gone for the last few days."

"You don't need to explain anything to me. The more the merrier."

I follow him out the door and down the hall. But rather than turn to go down the stairs, he takes me to the door just to the left of them. He knocks on the door and a small elderly woman answers. She has white hair that is cropped close to her head and curled. My guess is she looks to be almost one hundred. Her eyes light up when she sees Rice. When she notices me her mouths turns up to reveal a gummy smile. Rice grasps her hand and kisses her on her cheek. He whispers into her ear in Spanish. This man is full of surprises. She turns and walks away only to return a few seconds later to hand him some keys. Her tan and withered hand comes up to pat his cheek. Then she grabs my hand and puts it into his free one. I glance up at Rice and he just smiles at me and then leans down and gives her another kiss on the cheek. Bernie has pushed his way through our clasped hands. The little old woman pets his face and he gives her a couple of slobbery kisses. Judging by the way his tail is wagging he knows her and is very fond of her.

Rice pulls Bernie back and following his lead I head towards the stairs. She watches us until we are out of sight and then I hear her door click shut. When we exit the building, I follow Rice over to a champagne color old model four-door Dodge. It is the quintessential old lady car. Taking the keys she gave him he unlocks the passenger side door for me. Before I can get in Bernie hops in and sits in the middle. His enthusiasm makes me laugh and I follow him in. Rice walks around the car and climbs in the driver side.

"Who was that?"

He starts the car and pulls out onto the street before answering, "That is Ms. Benitez. When I first moved in she was trying to climb the stairs with all her groceries by herself. I offered to help her. We've watched out for each other ever since. She watches Bernie sometimes. I'm pretty sure he likes her more than he likes me." Glancing around Bernie and over at me he smiles, "He seems to like the fairer sex better and I can't say I blame him." He leans back and continues, "She's all alone. So I do chores and errands for her and in return she makes me home cooked meals."

If it's at all possible, I think I fall a little more in love with him. "You really are one of the good ones, aren't you?"

His face hardens a little before smoothing into a small grin, "I try to be, but I still have my naughty side." The little wink and the implication of his words send a shiver down my spine.

We continue on our drive in comfortable silence. Bernie is leaning his head over mine to try to get to the window. After a few minutes his self-control gives out and he climbs over me to put his head out. I just smile and lean my head on his side.

Rice pulls up in front of a warehouse and puts the car in park. I follow him inside and am hit with the mouthwatering smell of coffee. Lights click on and Bernie runs ahead of us to what I'm assuming is an office. When I finally get there I see Rice unlocking a cabinet in the corner. When he opens it, I'm shocked to see an arsenal. There are big guns and little guns. Knives upon knives are lined along the door. Baffled how anyone could ever have a need or a use for so many weapons I remember that Rice is part of the mafia.

It's so easy to forget everything when I'm with him. The world sort of fades away. When he's done stocking up, he locks the cabinet and approaches me with a small gun in his hand and inquires, "Have you ever fired a gun?" When I shake my head he places the gun in my hand and says, "This is a Smith and Wesson M & P Shield."

I've never held a gun before. My heart beats a little faster and in a mixture of panic and adrenaline I retort, "I don't think the type of gun or the name of it really matters here, do you? It's not going to help me suddenly know how to shoot."

He chortles as he continues, "No, it probably doesn't." As he is talking he comes behind me and placing his hands around mine brings the gun up into shooting position, "There isn't a safety so you just have to chamber the bullet and then point and shoot. To chamber the bullet you pull back on the slide, which is this," he motions to the top back portion of the gun, "There is a little bit of a kick when you shoot but nothing too bad." He steps back and I'm left holding the gun.

"Rice, I really don't think this is necessary. I will probably kill or hurt myself before I even hit whatever is coming at me." I try to hand it back to him.

"Imogen, you are taking the gun. No arguing. I won't have you unarmed given the current situation. If I knew where you were holed up for the last few days I'm sure he knows too and if not he's probably found out."

The thought that Michael might have known where I was this entire time makes my blood run cold. Then the realization of what Rice just said has my skin flaming with embarrassment.

I croak, "You. You've known where I've been this whole time? You were watching and spying on me?" Memories from my time with Calder are flashing through my mind. I'm not sure why but the thought of Rice knowing what happened with Calder is making my stomach turn. Luckily his response calms me down.

"No, I wasn't watching you. I knew the FBI had you and that you would be safe with them. But I stayed close and kept a look out."

"Oh, oh that's good then."

"Back to the gun, you're taking it. I won't let there be a reason for you to have to use it but if something happens to me I have to know that you will have a chance at protecting yourself. Promise me that if you have to use it you will?"

I gulp down the nerves and agree, "I promise."

"Good girl." Straightening he says, "Now let's go get Mr. Darcy and," he pauses, "Cleo? Who is Cleo?"

"Yes, Cleo. Cleo is the baby duck I rescued," I beam.

"I should have known. It's a good thing you were only there for a couple days. Otherwise you'd have a whole zoo by the time I got to you." Reaching for my hand he adds, "Let's go." He starts to head out into the warehouse and I realize that once we leave here reality will come crashing back. There is someone out there who wants to kill me and right now I'm not sure I'm ready to pop this little delusional idea that I'm in a safety bubble here with Rice.

"Actually, I was wondering if you could show me how you roast the coffee. I've never seen it done before and I'm really curious," I hurry. I know I should be racing to get to Mr. Darcy and Cleo but I can't help my desire to keep Rice here all to myself. "I mean, does it take a long time?"

"No, it doesn't take a long time, maybe about an hour from start to finish. And I would love to show you around." He sets the keys down on his desk and grabs the gun and does the same with it. Then he leads me out into the main warehouse. I didn't get a good look when I first walked in but this place is massive. It could easily be split into two separate warehouses and each warehouse would have plenty of space.

We pass a small kitchen that is along the wall off to the right side. There are some shelves with different utensils, bowls, and things off to the left just past the door we entered from. We keep walking farther into the center of the room. All along the walls is exposed brick and the floor is a stained and sealed concrete. The roasting machines are against the wall on the right. To say they are huge would be an understatement. Way bigger than I had imagined them being. There are four of them and they are black and stainless steel. Separating the machines and the small kitchen are stacks of barrels. Off to the left are rows and rows of huge burlap bags filled with coffee beans. They are all stamped with the name "Finca De Café." There are a couple trucks and a delivery van marked with Mezzanote Coffee Co. Farther past them it looks like another office and a few more rooms. I start to wonder if it really was two warehouses that they combined into one. There are a couple of garage doors where the trucks and vans can pull out. On the other side of the cars I can just make out what looks like stacks and rows of more coffee beans.

"Wow. I didn't realize you guys were this big. I mean your coffee is the best but this, this is impressive."

"Thanks, we're growing every day. But we actually do more than just sell roasted coffee."

"Oh, that's right, like, illegal things?" I ask, half afraid of his answer.

"No," he reminds me, "You're dad is getting out of the illegal *things* remember? We supply other roasters with coffee beans from our farm. This place almost couldn't be any more perfect. We get our beans come from Mexico and it's almost a straight shot here to Louisiana. That's what those are," he says pointing to the stacks and stacks of bags of coffee beans on the other side of the cars, "We take and deliver and mail those to coffee roasting companies around the country. Then they roast them themselves, like Mezzanote. Mezzanote is doing really well, in fact your dad is looking into possibly opening a second roasting facility back in Boston. We weren't planning on keeping this one down here long term but it's becoming profitable, so he'll probably keep it." My hopes soar at the thought of him being here permanently. They are destroyed just as quickly when he continues, "Once things settle here I'll go home to Boston and help get the facility up there put together."

All I can manage is nodding my head up and down awkwardly. Unaware of my awkwardness he states, "Let's roast some coffee. First we grab the bag of coffee beans." He then goes over and grabs one of the bags from a pile and carries it over to the roasting machine farthest from the office. He sets the bag down and turns on the machine. Raising his voice over the hum of the machine he continues, "Then we dump them in up here. From there, they filter down into the drum. They'll tumble around in there as they're roasted. This is the part that takes anywhere from ten to twenty minutes. To save some time we'll do a light roast. We just want to listen for the first crack and then the beans will dump out into the cooling bin. They'll be rotated and constantly moved by these metal arms. Once they are cooled we package them and send them on their way."

"I didn't realize it was so quick. So you do this every morning, and then you go around and deliver the freshly roasted beans? Or do they sit here at all," I yell over the sound of the beans tumbling.

"Yep, we deliver the beans right after we roast them. We also grind some up and sell pre-ground coffee."

I start doing the awkward nodding again until my eyes fall on the barrels so I inquire, "What do you do with those? They look like wine and liquor barrels. Are you guys going to start a winery and a distillery too?"

"Actually," he face lights up with pride as he continues, "that is my baby. Since coffee beans can actually start to take on the taste of things around them if exposed for long amounts of time, I had an idea. What if we used that to infuse the coffee beans with flavors that we wanted? Your dad has some connections and was able to get a deal on the empty used barrels. We take the green coffee beans and then seal them in the dry barrels. It takes a couple of months for the beans to fully absorb the flavor from the barrels. Our first batch is scheduled to be done in the next couple weeks, so we'll see how it goes."

"That is incredible," I trail off when I see he isn't paying attention to me anymore. He is listening to the side of the machine and smelling the air. Then he presses a button and the coffee beans come pouring out into the big round cooling pan. The clicking of coffee beans hitting each other and the sound of the air being forced through the machinery to cool the beans is noisy.

The metal arms stir the beans around in the pan for a few minutes. Then the beans pour down into a clean bucket. He turns the machine off, "And that's it, pretty easy and pretty easy to screw up. I did that a lot in the beginning. Now I do it mostly by smell, sound, and sight. Let's go get Mr. Darcy."

"What about the coffee beans? Don't we need to do something with them? They won't go bad sitting out like this?" I ask.

"No, they'll be fine. I'll come by later and deal with them," smiling, he grabs my hand. "Oh," he remembers, "I have to grab my keys." He's just picking up his keys when we both hear a noise come from somewhere in the warehouse.

All the blood rushes from my face when I see Bernie right next to us. I thought at first it was him who had made the noise but now that I know he's here with us it couldn't have been him. I know it is Michael. I can feel it in my bones. That feeling where you know something bad is going to happen, almost like that animalistic sixth sense. Worse is knowing I can't do anything to stop it. Rice grabs the gun and puts it in my hand then he grabs my shoulders and looks me in the eye as he insists, "Stay here. Lock the door after me. Keep the gun in your hand and chamber a bullet. Use it if you need to." Then he turns to Bernie and goes down on one knee. Looking in his eyes, he says sternly, "Stay. Keep her safe." Rice stands looks at me for a second before he pulls me into him and slams his mouth down on mine. He is out the door with a gun in his hands before I can even say anything.

I do as he told me to and lock the door. It seems like hours have gone by and I haven't heard anything. Glancing at a clock I realize it has only been five minutes. I look at Bernie and murmur, "Do you think he is going to be okay?" I know he can't really answer me but the silence is going to make me crazy. My mind is already coming up with a million different scenarios of how this is going to play out. "I mean I know I'm not the best back up but maybe the gun will help scare Michael away or maybe I can at the very least throw the gun at his face," I ramble to him. "I know. I know he said to stay here. And yes, I know he will be mad at me for leaving. But I can't leave him out there by himself. If he doesn't come back in the next five minutes, I'm going after him."

Bernie turns his head as he listens to me. I'm acutely aware of each click of the second hand on the clock. I'm focused on it that intensely. As soon as it hits the ten minute mark since Rice has been gone I fly up onto my feet. Turning to Bernie, I whisper, "Stay here. I'll be back."

I unlock the door and tip toe out. The gun is hanging, loosely at my side in my hand. I bring it up in front of me and into my chest like I see in the movies. If I don't know what I'm doing, at the very least I can look the part. When I get to the shelving on the left side I put my back up against it and peek around the side. I don't see anything so I use the next one as my cover as I peek around the corner of the shelf. There is no one and no sound in the warehouse other than the buzz from the lights and various appliances.

Stepping around the second shelf, I tip-toe farther into the warehouse.

A tingle starts in my neck a few seconds before I feel the cold metal gun barrel pressed into it. His voice is like acid to my stomach. "It really isn't nice to ditch your friends."

Icy cold fear trickles down my spine and steals my breath. I take a breath to answer him but before I get any words out I hear a deep menacing growl and feel a slight breeze and then Bernie has his mouth wrapped around Michael's arm.

Michael screams and starts flailing and kicking. "Get off me, you stupid mutt!" I spin around and bring my gun up to point at him. There is no way I can take a shot. In the best case scenario there is only a slim chance I hit Michael. That slim chance isn't worth the risk of hitting Bernie. If I did hit Bernie, I couldn't live with myself. I do the only thing I can think of and throw the whole gun at Michael. I've never been very athletic and I prove that as I miss him by a mile. Right as the gun hits the floor, Michael gets a hard kick right into Bernie's side. Bernie lets go of his arm and goes flying off and hits the edge of a shelf.

"No!" I bawl. I lunge for Bernie but Michael grabs me by my hair and yanks him to me. He spins me around in front of him and brings a gun up to my head just as Rice barrels around the delivery van. Rice's face falls when he sees me.

Michael yells at him, "Drop the gun!" Rice continues to hold the gun pointed at Michael. Michael raises the gun over his head and pulls the trigger.

Throwing his hands up in surrender, Rice lowers and drops the gun to the floor and kicks it away with his foot. "Okay, okay, just don't hurt her," he pleads.

"That's better. Oh and I'm not planning on hurting her." Then he adds, "Yet." He pushes the end of the gun into my temple.

I can barely hear what they are saying over the pounding of my heart in my ears. My vision is blurry from the tears that are streaming down my face. I'm locking eyes with Rice when he soothingly says, "Imogen. Look at my eyes. Everything is going to be okay."

"Oh, shut up, you liar," smirks Michael. "You know as well as I do that, first, I'm going to kill you. Then I'm going to make sure your dog is dead. The stupid mangy mutt *ruined* my new jacket. Then I'm taking little miss precious here and turning her in for a lot of money." He leans down and whispers in my ear,

"Girl, you weren't kidding about him. I could eat him up all day long. If he played on my team I might be able to forgive him for shooting me in the thigh." A wave of nausea wracks my body at the feel of his breath on my neck. During his tirade he keeps leaning forward towards Rice, which is moving us closer to him. It isn't nearly close enough but maybe if he keeps talking.

I haven't been paying attention to anything except Rice's eyes, but it looks like he's been moving forward closer to us to. Michael must not have noticed because he hasn't said or done anything. There is a throbbing in my side and above my knee and I know that my cuts from the other day have opened up again. Rice is still looking me in the eye which is why I see the small shift of his eyes and the almost imperceptible nod of his head.

Then he begs as he moves forward even more, "Just let her go. Then you can go. If you let her go I promise I won't hurt you."

Michael barks out a laugh. "You aren't in a position to beg for anything. Although, I do like the thought of you in a different position begging me for something else."

The next moments seem to happen in fast forward and slow motion all at the same time. There is a shout from behind us.

"FBI, arms up." My heart stops at the sound of his voice. At the same time Rice lunges forward and grabs and pulls me towards him. Michael turns towards the voice. As he turns, the hand that was holding the gun to my head lowers and the gun goes off. I feel a burning sensation tear across my right butt cheek. Rice pulls me down to the ground underneath him. There are more shots fired and then everything is silent except the ringing in my ears from the sound of the gunshots.

Rice rolls me over and takes my face in his hands. My voice morphs into a cringe when I hit where Michael's bullet tore through my butt cheek. His face filled with worry, he runs his hands down my arms and legs while he scans my body for the source of the pain. He sighs in relief when he sees the only thing wrong with me is a few inches of missing fat. Tears fill my eyes as I look into his and whisper, "Bernie?" His head turns to his dog and I nod at his unasked question. Leaving me he goes over to Bernie.

Propping myself up on my elbow, I see his face buried into Bernie's neck fur and I choke on a sob. I almost miss the little lift of Bernie's head through my tear-filled eyes. My sobs turn from heartbroken to elated in seconds. I unsuccessfully try to avoid seeing Michael. When I heard those gunshots I knew what the outcome was going to be. His still body is lying just in front of me. Suddenly my view is blocked and Calder is there.

I'm wrapped in his strong arms and I grab onto his broad shoulders. The moment lasts less than a minute before the warehouse is full of people in FBI vests and paramedics are rushing in. The silence from a few seconds ago is now clamorous chaos. Calder reluctantly lets me go and stands up to talk to the people filling the warehouse. Two paramedics approach me and my eyes seek out Rice only he isn't there. He's vanished along with Bernie.

The paramedics sit next to me and start taking my vitals and assessing my injuries. I'm trying to see around them to find Calder. He is talking with some man in a suit who, judging by his demeanor is probably his boss. I catch his eye for only a brief second before he is leading the suit guy around.

- Rice -

I can't stand the fact that I left her in my office alone. There's a feeling in the pit of my stomach that she isn't going to stay put and that I might have just made another huge mistake. It's too late now as I silently creep through the warehouse. I'm looking around corners and piles of coffee beans. Not seeing anything in this section, I move through the vehicles that are parked and after not finding anything again I move to the huge stacks of coffee beans on this side.

I've made it half way down the first stack when I hear a growl and then his voice starts yelling. My stomach drops as I turn and run back as fast as I can. Not getting to her isn't an option. I'm holding out slight hope that maybe, just maybe, he hasn't found her and that Bernie was protecting her. Rounding the corner, all hopes are dashed when I see him with his hands wrapped around her and a gun pointed at her temple. They are standing in front and to the side of some shelving.

I hear him yell at me to drop the gun. Glancing down I see I have my gun trained on him. I don't even remember bringing it up and aiming it at him. I wasn't fast enough for his liking because he raises the gun and takes a warning shot. My arms fly up and I set the gun on the ground and kick out of the way while pleading, "Okay, okay, just please don't hurt her."

He responds back to me, "That's better. Oh and I'm not planning on hurting her." He pauses, "Yet."

I lock onto Imogen's eyes, focus only on her and say, "Imogen. Look at my eyes. Everything is going to be okay."

He scoffs at me, "Oh, shut up, you liar. You know as well as I do that, first, I'm going to kill you. Then I'm going to make sure your dog is dead." At the mention of Bernie, I notice his still form on the ground in front of the shelves. While he is talking, I'm slowly shuffling forward to get closer to them. "The stupid mangy mutt *ruined* my new jacket. Then I'm taking little miss precious here and turning her in for a lot of money." He whispers something in Imogen's ear and I can see the disgust on her face. I notice that during his little rant he has moved closer to me too.

A movement behind them catches my attention. I barely allow my eyes to flick to see what is there since I don't want to give anything away. Calder is coming up behind Michael with his gun raised. With an undetected nod of my head, I signal that I see him. I know I'm not quite close enough to grab her so I need to find a way to close the distance.

Going for begging, I say, "Just let her go. Then you can go. If you let her go, I promise I won't hurt you." In my head I add, because you can't hurt when you're dead. But he doesn't know that.

He responds with a laugh, "You aren't in a position to beg for anything. Although, I do like the thought of you in a different position, begging me for something else."

Calder and I synchronize our attacks. He shouts, "FBI, arms up," at the same time I lunge forward and manage to grab Imogen and pull her towards me. I hear a gun go off and I'm not sure which one it is. More shots are fired as our momentum drives us to the ground and I twist Imogen underneath me. Rolling her over I take her face in my hands and relief floods me. It's in that moment that I know I love her. I don't have a right to but I can't help it. Her face fills with pain and panic once again floods me. I run my hands down her arms and legs checking for wounds. When I realize she was hit in the butt cheek and that it is more of a skimming I calm down.

Her eyes suddenly fill with tears and she whispers, "Bernie?" I turn to look at his body and when I look back at her she nods, answering the question I didn't need to ask.

Leaving her, I'm full of trepidation as I walk over to Bernie and crouch down. I can see his chest rising and falling and my head falls into his neck fur. He lifts his head a little and lays it back down. Turning, I glance back at Imogen and see Calder take her into an intimate embrace. Pushing the sudden flood of jealousy aside, I gather Bernie into my arms and make my way to the door and to the car. I need to get Bernie to the vet to get checked out. I would stay and make sure Imogen is okay but she seems to be in more than capable hands.

- Calder -

I've been a mess ever since he took her. Thinking back to that day, I remember blacking out and waking up when the paramedics started working on me. I was pretty lucky since the shot to my side just skimmed me and the one to my shoulder was more towards the outside and hit mostly muscle. They still hurt like a bitch. I can handle that pain. The pain I can't handle is the thought that something has happened to her, that I wasn't able to keep her safe. They made me go to the hospital to get stitched up and checked out. The argument with my boss about how I'm not taking leave and that I'm going after her was intense and long but I eventually won. There's something to be said for being a stubborn ass.

I went and visited Imogen's friend Kelly, and then June and Mabel at the retirement home. Neither visit produced anything useful. I was starting to feel a little defeated until I got information yesterday that Michael had been spotted.

That leads us to right now and me following him into some industrial part of town. I'm breaking about a million rules and laws right now since I should immediately reported the information I found. But I couldn't risk him slipping away again which is why I have been following him since last night.

He pulls into a big solitary warehouse and parks. I make a quick call asking for backup and giving them my location. After waiting a few minutes to make sure he hasn't realized he was followed, I take out my gun and follow him in. My shoulder burns as I use the muscles that are trying to heal and my wound stretches.

Not wanting to give away my position, I go to a window on the side of the building and peek through. I see what looks to be an empty office. Trying the windows I'm relieved when one of them is open. Crawling through the window, I hear a gunshot. My instincts have me crouching and listening but my heart and gut want to rush in there to protect the woman I care about. Creeping out of the office, I see that he has her in front of him with a gun next to her head. Maurice "Rice" Fitzpatrick is standing in front of them with his arms up in surrender.

I don't have time to feel like an idiot that I didn't realize this was Mezzanote's warehouse and that I didn't know Rice was here. Just more proof that my mind hasn't been focused since taking this assignment. My focus has been on her when it should have been on how to keep her safe. I can beat myself up later; right now I have to focus on getting Imogen out of Michael's arms. Rice's eyes meet mine and I see an almost unnoticeable head nod. I take that as a signal and wait for a cue.

Rice moves closer to Michael and Imogen as he begs him to let Imogen go. Michael laughs and responds, "You aren't in a position to beg for anything. Although I do like the thought of you in a different position, begging me for something else."

I take that as my cue and yell, "FBI, arms up!" Rice lunges for Imogen at the same time and pulls her away from Michael. Michael twists towards me and his gun goes off. I fire several shots at him and he falls.

I make my way over to him and kick his gun away. I bend down and check his vitals and confirm what I already knew. He's dead. Looking at his body, I see I hit him right in the heart. I'm proud of my hit but also disappointed that he didn't suffer. The little prick should have suffered hours and hours of agonizing pain for what he's done to her.

Standing up, I look over as Rice leaves Imogen and moves to a dog that is lying on the ground. I hadn't even noticed the dog was there. Shit, I'm off my game. My eyes shift back to Imogen and I see her sobs and run to her. My arms wrap around her and my heart lifts that she is safe and in my arms. I realize that I don't just care for Imogen but that I'm falling in love with her. She is everything that I never knew I wanted and needed. The feeling scares the piss out of me. Luckily I'm saved from further self-evaluation. Back up arrives and the warehouse is flooded with people.

I leave her and motion to the paramedics to check her out. My boss is walking in and I know that this isn't going to be a fun or a short conversation.

CHAPTER THIRTEEN

- Imogen -

I'm forced to go to the hospital for my injuries. My cuts need stitches as does the bullet wound on my butt. They are also afraid I might have a concussion from where Michael hit me with the gun and that I may be dehydrated. So I'm awarded a very uncomfortable bumpy ride to the hospital in an ambulance.

When I get to the hospital, they give me some pain medicine before they clean my wounds. Then I have to sit through the uncomfortable sensation of my numb skin being pulled and tugged. I'm definitely not a fan of stitches. It's about two hours later when they finally wheel me up to my own room. I'm started on fluids and antibiotics to prevent infection since the cuts from Michael have opened up a few times and been left exposed.

The pain medication has kicked in and, the crash from the adrenaline rush has left me exhausted. I'm almost asleep when I hear intense arguing right outside my room. All of a sudden June comes charging through the door followed by nervous nurses and an embarrassed Mabel. She runs up to me and wraps me up in a huge comforting bear hug. Sitting next to me, and she takes my hand, in hers and jumps right into her story.

"Oh, Immy! I've been so worried about you. Kelly told me you went on a romantic getaway. At first I was so excited for you. Finally you were enjoying life and having some fun! But then I hadn't heard from you and I started to get worried. Then not yesterday but the day before this very handsome young man shows up at the home waving a badge around and saying he's FBI. It was the most exciting thing to happen since Norma got that STD. I wouldn't be surprised if Leroy had a heart attack from all the excitement. Anyway, back to my story. So he comes in and wants to see Mabel and me. Obviously I think he's probably a lunatic but he was very good looking so I turn to Mabel and say, 'He's a lot cuter in person than he is in his picture on the internet'," she pauses for a second to laugh at the memory of her joke. Then she continues, "Oh you should have seen old Bertie when I said that! So he comes over to us and tells us this crazy story. It's something you would

239

see in the movies! About how your dad is a mafia boss who is being blackmailed by a drug lord and they had to take you into protective custody. Then you were kidnapped and they were trying to find you. Once we realized it wasn't some prank we started demanding they find you. You should have seen Mabel," at this part she motions her head towards Mabel, who is standing on the other side of the bed. "She was up in his face screaming at him. I didn't know she had it in her. You should have seen his poor face! He told us they were doing everything that they could and that if we hear anything or think of anything that could help that we let them know. That was all we knew until about an hour ago when he called and told us where you were."

June hugs me again and Mabel reaches down and squeezes my hand. Mabel adds, "Oh Immy, we were so worried. I'm so glad you're alright."

I give her a reassuring squeeze, "I'm so glad you guys are here. I'm sorry to worry you." I try fighting my heavy eyelids. It keeps getting harder and harder to open them. I hear Mabel whisper to June.

"We should let her get some rest. We'll go down to the cafeteria."

They must leave because it's quiet and then the next thing I know I'm waking up and it's dark outside. June and Mabel are sitting in chairs watching the TV. They see me wake up and they both rush over to me. Mabel presses the nurses call button.

"How are you feeling, sweetheart?" June asks.

"Did you get some good sleep? Do you need anything? The nurse told us to call them when you wake up," Mabel informs me.

"I'm good. I'm a little sore and I'm actually really thirsty. Do you think I could get some water?"

The nurse comes in then and asks how I'm doing. I repeat what I just told June and Mabel. She types some information into her screen and then asks about my pain and if I'm ready for some more pain medicine. When I give her an enthusiastic, "Yes," she smiles. She takes my blood pressure and temperature and enters them into her computer. A room service menu is put into my hand and she explains how to order and then she leaves. A cup of water and a little paper cup with some pills in it are in her hands when she comes back. Then she tells me to buzz her if I need anything and she leaves.

Looking at my choices, I notice that they close at 8:00 p.m. I only have ten minutes to get my order in. Hurriedly, I pick a grilled cheese sandwich with macaroni and cheese, a dinner roll, and some chilled apple crisp thing for dessert. After placing my order, I lean back in my bed and look at June and Mabel standing off to the side. I smile when I see they are arguing with each other. Straining to hear what they are saying, I can only make out a few snippets. 'Don't you dare ask her,' and, 'I want to know what happened to her,' and, 'Don't make her relive it,' followed by, 'What if something happened with that hunky FBI agent?' Deciding to put June out of her misery and dispel any discomfort Mabel feels I ask, "So, are you guys ready to hear what happened?'

June grabs a chair and pulls it over, eager for me to start. Mabel, still being the sensitive one, reassures me, "Oh, Immy, you don't need to relive the horrible experience. You just get some rest. We are happy just sitting here knowing you are safe. If you want to talk about it later you can."

"Thanks, Mabel, but it really is fine. Plus if I didn't tell you, then you would never know what happened with the hunky FBI agent," I tease. June's eyes light up and I wink at her and then continue, "So it started the day of your contest," and I gesture to June. "I came back and the lights were on in the front of the café, which isn't too unusual when Kelly closes up since she forgets sometimes. Anyway, so I head up to the front and see she has left me a note. I read it and then turn to flip the lights off but I hear something and a man has come through the front door. Well, I think he probably thought we were open so I explain it to him and go to show him out the door and I see he has a gun and it's pointed at me! I panic and then hear a something that sounds like a loud crack and fall backwards. At this point I think he has shot me but I can't feel any pain. I convince myself that I don't feel pain because my body is in shock. Which after getting this, shock my ass," and I motion to my butt cheek, "You can definitely feel it. Anyway, back to the story. So then this face pops up in front of my face and I think it's the man and he is going to do horrible horrible things to me so I start kicking and hitting, basically flailing all over the place. It turns out to be Calder, who is the FBI guy who actually is Wall Street. Remember me telling you about him? Anyway, the sound I heard was him killing the other guy. Then he tells me he's taking me to a safe house."

There is a slight knock on my door so I stop my story while they drop off my dinner. Once they leave again I continue. "I tell him I'm not going anywhere without Mr. Darcy," I gasp as I think about him and realize he is probably still stuck at the cabin. Frantically I exclaim, "Mr. Darcy! He's still at the cabin! I have to get out of here. I have to get him." I try to get up and realize I am attached by a few tubes and cords. My hands fly to try to rid me of them just as June breaks in.

"Imogen! Mr. Darcy is fine. Calder, that was his name right? Calder brought him when he went to talk to Kelly. He talked to her first since he remembered you had called her. She has Mr. Darcy and he is okay. Oh and that reminds me, you are supposed to call her as soon as you wake up. But you can call her after you finish your story. I can tell you were just getting to the good part!"

Relief washes over me at the news that Mr. Darcy is okay and has been taken care of. Finding out Calder thought to take care of him and go back for him does funny things to my heart. As I let the breath out I was holding I say, "Oh. That's good. Okay, yes I'll call Kelly after I eat."

Picking up my sandwich I take a bite of food and resume talking through my bite. "So where was I? Oh yeah. I told him I wouldn't leave Mr. Darcy so we go upstairs to grab my some of my stuff and Mr. Darcy." I narrow my eyes at Mabel, "Where Darcy just so happened to be chewing on the Christmas present you got us all last year, so thanks for that."

She blushes with embarrassment. I smile to let her know I'm joking then I continue, "There wasn't another safe house ready so we went to Calder's grandfather's cabin. We were there for a couple days." I smile and get a dreamy look on my face when I think about our time spent at the cabin. "We talked and got to know each other. He taught me how to fish. Oh, and I found an orphaned baby duck! So does Kelly have Cleo too?" I ask.

"Who is Cleo? Kelly didn't mention a Cleo."

That is odd. I wonder what Calder did with her. "Cleo is the baby duck. I wonder where she is. Maybe Calder kept her? He had better not just let her go or I'll kill him." I shake my head and continue my story, "So we found the duck and then we had to go and find food to feed her, so we went into town to find food. We stopped at the pet store and I called Kelly and left her a message telling her I was okay. Then we went to the grocery store and that is where I ran into Michael. He grabbed me and shot Calder. I was knocked out and woke up tied to a chair. He tried to get me to talk on the phone to someone to confirm I was there but I wouldn't and then he gave me these," and I point to my cuts. "Rice came and saved me. Rice, the coffee roaster I buy my coffee from, Rice. Who actually it turns out is someone my dad sent to keep an eye on me. So basically all the hot men that come into my life are either federal agents,

245

hit men, or part of the mafia. No wonder I've been single for so long."

I push my tray away when I'm finished with my dinner and finish my story. "So Rice rescues me and shoots Michael in the thigh as we are escaping. We have to spend the night in the woods. Then, get this, in the morning Rice goes and catches some fish for us to eat all MacGyver style with a soda can tab and some string from this thing around his wrist! After we eat the fish we have to hike out which takes forever with me limping and the cuts hurting. We stole a car. Went to his apartment, only at first I thought it was someone else's apartment and we were going to have to whack him. You know because that is what the mafia does." At this June is enthusiastically nodding her head. "But we don't because it is Rice's apartment, his name is actually Maurice. We stay there that night. We go to get Mr. Darcy the next day but we have to stop and get guns from Rice's roasting warehouse. Then Michael shows up and then Calder shows up and kills him and then you know the rest."

I sit back and take stock of their shocked faces. June is the first one to talk and all she wants is to ask, "So what happened during all of those *nights* you were alone with two very attractive, virile men?"

A blush creeps up my chest and neck and onto my cheeks. Sheepishly I answer, "Well, actually, I did kiss both of them."

June asks incredulously, "Kiss? You only kissed them?"

Laughing, I respond, "Yes, only a kiss. But," I pause for dramatic effect, "they were pretty incredible kisses. Not that it matters now anyway. Calder will get his big promotion he's been waiting for and move to Washington, D.C., Rice will go back to Boston to take over for my dad. And I'll be left here single. But such is life, c'est la vie."

I notice it's getting late so I tell them they need to go home and I'll see them tomorrow. It takes some arguing and convincing but eventually they relent and leave. I'm getting tired again and decide to hurry and call Kelly before I fall asleep. She shrieks when she hears my voice and then proceeds to yell at me, "IMOGEN CORDELIA JONES, if you EVER, and I mean EVER, scare me like that again I will kill you myself!"

"I'm sorry, Kel. I couldn't tell you the truth. But I'm okay now. Thanks for watching Mr. Darcy for me. I'm pretty exhausted so I'm going to go to bed but I wanted to call you before so you didn't worry anymore."

"I know you couldn't tell me the truth and I'm only half

kidding. You know I'll watch Mr. Darcy anytime you need me to. Thanks for calling me and now get some sleep because I'm seeing you tomorrow and then you are telling me the whole story. Love you, Imms. You're the jelly to my peanut butter."

"Love you too, Kel. You're the peanut butter to my jelly," I finish as I hang up the phone.

I'm disappointed that neither Calder nor Rice came to see me. You would think after my safety being both of their jobs for the last little while they would want to make sure I was okay. I know I've been telling myself to not get attached, that both of them will be leaving and to just enjoy the time we've had. But, like the idiot I am, I developed feelings for not only one of them, but both of them. Maybe it's a good thing neither of them came. It probably would have made it harder when they left again. I fall asleep dreaming of both of them.

CHAPTER FOURTEEN

- Imogen -

I wake up slowly and a little disoriented. My eyes fall on Calder sitting in a chair opposite me.

When he sees that I'm awake he gives me a smile. "Hey."

"Hi," I respond a little sheepishly. There's a small flutter in my stomach as I take him in. He's dressed in a gray suit with a gray-blue dress shirt and a navy tie. His face is clean shaven and his hair is done. He looks like he did when he first came into The Artful Blend.

Standing up he walks over to me. "I was just coming to let you know that everything has been taken care of. Your life can go back to normal. Your dad's testimony was enough to convict Manuel Rodriguez. There's a minor threat of retaliation so local PD will keep an eye out for the next couple of weeks. And, off the record, your dad has some tricks up his sleeve to prevent any further retaliation against you or anyone else in his family or employ."

"Tricks, huh? Like super-secret mafia tricks," I tease.

"Something like that," he says through a smile. Then he adds, "Your dad has a lot of information on a lot of bad people. Knowledge is power. He made it known that if anything happens to him or anyone associated with him that those secrets will be made public and available to the US government. None of them want that, so you'll be safe."

"Oh, well, that's good. So I guess you'll be leaving now," I surmise.

"I'm actually on my way to the airport. I just wanted to come by and let you know that the case was closed and that you're going to be fine."

Fine isn't the word I would use to describe what I'm going to be. But his sentiment is right, I'll live. I have June, Mabel, and Kelly. I might not have someone there at night or by my side, well, not a human someone. I'll always have Mr. Darcy there. I look around and then focus back on him, "Well, thanks. Have a safe flight."

"Take care, Imogen," he says tenderly as he bends over and

kisses my forehead. He turns and starts walking to the door and then suddenly whips around, "Oh, I almost forgot. This is from your dad. He can't travel yet or he would have been down here. He wanted you to get this."

I take the letter from his hands and gulp down my trepidation at reading the letter. "Bye, Calder." My eyes are fixed on the letter in my hands but I hear him start for the door when I remember something I wanted to ask him. "Calder? Where's Cleo? June told me Kelly had Mr. Darcy but she didn't know anything about Cleo."

He turns around and a slight blush creeps up his neck as he answers, "Here's the thing." Struggling with trying to find the wording he wants, he finally rushes, "I got attached to her and I couldn't imagine letting her go. So I kept her. If that's okay."

And just like that, I fall even more in love with him. A huge smile breaks across my face, "That's good. I think she liked you better anyway."

He gives a nod and, looking me over a few times, says, "See you around, Imogen." Then he is gone.

My eyes sting as they slowly fill with tears. I'm trying desperately to memorize his face and my name on his lips and commit to them to memory.

The doctor walks in and I hurriedly wipe my eyes. He asks how I'm feeling and then explains the medications he's sending me home with. Everything is happening in a blur and I'm not paying attention to what he's saying. Then he leaves and they prepare me for discharge.

I hurry and call Kelly and ask if she can come and pick me up. She agrees. I call June and, she takes some convincing, but she finally relents to letting Kelly pick me up since she hasn't heard the whole story yet.

"Holy mother," Kelly says in disbelief. We made it to my apartment from the hospital, and we're lying on my bed. I just finished telling her the events of the last week. "I'm in shock. Complete and utter shock. You could have died! And Michael?! He was our best friend, Imm. We shared everything with him. And then they both just leave you?!" She lays back and shakes her head.

"Pretty much. But I'm just going to look at it that I was lucky enough to live a bad action movie *and* I got to make out with two gorgeous amazing guys. I mean, how many people do you know who can say that?" I ask her. "So the doctor said I'm not allowed to work for a week but what he doesn't know won't hurt him. I'm planning on being back tomorrow."

"Are you out of your freaking mind?" she screams at me. "There is no way in hell I'm allowing you into that kitchen until the week is up. And that is final!"

"Yes, mother," I tease. Turning serious, I tell her, "Kel, thank you. Thanks for being here for me and just for everything. You're my soul mate and I'll love you for always."

"Ahhh, I love you too."

She stays for another hour and we munch on some chips and guacamole. I'm left alone in my bed when she leaves and Mr. Darcy curls up next to me. Five chick flicks later, I'm out for the count.

The next day is nice and relaxing. It's nice to be able to lounge around watching movies and binging on Netflix. The police officers in charge of keeping an eye on me come by and introduce themselves. Joe is older, in his mid fifties. He's married and his youngest just went off to college. Mack is younger and in his thirties and he just proposed to his girlfriend. Mr. Darcy is being needy and won't leave my side. He's probably scared I'll disappear again.

Apparently one day of down time is enough because I'm

about to go stir crazy. I feel like I've already watched every single movie I own. Given the doctor's orders I can't even pass the time with cleaning and organizing my apartment. Who I'm kidding I wouldn't be doing that even if the doctor said I could. I keep the café and its kitchen cleaned and organized but everything else is a disheveled mess. What I really want to do is bake. Baking is my release. Some people like running, some people like yoga, I like cracking eggs and mixing flour. It helps clear my head and then if it doesn't at least I get cupcakes in the end. That's another way I deal with stress. I'm definitely an emotional eater. Kelly won't let me so much as open the door to the café so going and baking down there is out of the question. I guess I'll have to make do with my small little cramped kitchen up here.

I'm just stuffing a second cupcake in my mouth when Joe and Mack stop by. I wrap up the rest of the cupcakes and pawn them off on them. Baking hasn't managed to clear my head and, given the whole emotional eating thing, it's probably better that I don't have two dozen cupcakes within arm's reach. I tell them there will be more tomorrow and to come prepared.

After they leave I watch a couple more movies before I call June. She's been calling every day to check on me. I told her she doesn't need to stop by since Kelly has been checking on me every day before and after running the café. Nobody pries about the letter from my dad. They all know it's sitting in my dresser and I haven't opened it yet. It's sitting there burning a hole in the drawer. I've pulled it out a couple times but I haven't gotten the courage to read it.

The next couple days are a blur of baking, movies, and Netflix, anything to keep my mind off the letter and Rice and Calder. I'm priding myself on the fact that over the last few days I've managed to only think about them a couple hundred times. Thinking about them spurs another round of baking. Thank goodness for Joe and Mack, otherwise you'd have to roll me out of my door by the time this week is up.

It's the night before I am cleared to go back to work that I finally get the courage to read the letter. The majority of the letter is him telling me how proud he is of who I have become and what I've accomplished. He apologizes for not being there while I was growing up, especially when my mom died. I'd never really thought about all that he missed out on. He never got to see me take my first steps or hear my first word. He missed dance recitals and soccer games. I always was curious as to he was. Do I look like him? Was he nice? I never had this aching yearning to figure out who he was though. I had everything I needed with my mom and then June and Mabel.

I've had my whole life to get used to the idea that he wasn't there. It was just a fact and not something I dwelled on. He's only had a year to get over that disappointment. I can't imagine the feeling of missing out on watching your child grow up. He doesn't have any expectations and it's up to me if I want a relationship with him. He wants to get to know me and be a part of my life but understands if that isn't something I want.

I've read and reread the letter a dozen times and I still don't know what I want to do. On the one hand I want to get to know my father and my half sister. But, in light of recent events, I don't know if I want to get any more connected to that world. I talk to June about it. I don't want her to feel like I don't appreciate all she's done for me and given me. I have never felt unwanted or unloved growing up. I've never really felt like I was missing anything. I don't want her to feel like she hasn't been enough. Of course she tells me I'm crazy for even thinking about that. She just wants me to be happy and she'll support whatever decision I make. Rice being so connected to them doesn't help with my decision. I want to see him again but I don't know if my heart can handle it. I know I need to make a decision but I think I'm going to bury my head in the sand for a little while longer.

Two Weeks Later

This morning is busy at the café and I'm still a little stiff and sore, so I'm relieved when Kelly comes walking in. She comes over and starts helping customers so I can go and get some more pastries from the back. As I'm walking out of the kitchen with my arms full with pans of muffins and croissants, I'm frozen in shock at the person who just walked through the door.

Calder looks even better than in he does in my dreams. He's in a pair of dark gray slacks and a white button up shirt. My eyes scan his body and my mind is trying to convince itself that this is real and not another dream. That first week back at the café I would catch myself watching the door waiting for him to walk in, but he never did, it wasn't until my eyes closed at night that he would finally come through the door. His eyes catch mine and his mouth splits into a mischievous and happy grin. Luckily Kelly sees me frozen staring at him and she comes over and grabs the trays out of my arms. Calder stopped right inside of the door when I saw him, now he starts to walk towards me as he says, "Hey."

I'm sure I look like a fish. My mouth is opening and closing as I try to find the right words to say. I finally manage to stutter, "How?"

"Can we sit and talk for a minute?" He motions me over to a table. I follow him over and once we sit down he answers, "There was an opening in the New Orleans office, a supervisor position. So I took it. I've been finding a place to live and moving my stuff down the last week."

Confusion wrinkles my brow, "But wait, I thought you were going to D.C., to be in the thick of things. Out in the field, in the big leagues. That was your dream."

"Dreams change. I think the fresh air up at the cabin helped clear my head. It also gave me some time to think. Plus it's not just about me anymore. I have Cleo to think about. It wouldn't be very nice of me to take her from a very spacious cabin near a river and her family to a cramped apartment in D.C. That's if I could even find an apartment in D.C. that would allow ducks."

"Are you a crazy person? Did you hit your head? Every conversation we've had you've talked about D.C. and how everything has been about the fastest way to get there. And then suddenly over night things just change? You can't just change your entire life's path because of a duck."

"Cleo, she has a name and she isn't just a duck, she's my duck." I smile when he throws my words back at me. He continues, "And like I told you, I started thinking about it at the cabin. I realized I missed it, being up there and out in nature. You know getting shot also has a way of putting things into perspective. This is where I want to be." Not giving me time to argue he presses a kiss to my forehead. "I'll be seeing you." And with that he walks away.

I have a dazed look on my face as I try to process everything that just happened. Making my way towards the kitchen I motion to Kelly that I am heading to my office. I need a minute after that conversation. I'm still in shock by Calder's sudden appearance which is why I don't see Rice leaning against the doorway of my office. Just like I watched and waited for Calder, I held out hope that first delivery that he would be the one making it. But the eighteen year old kid who came in dashed those hopes fast. The only time I've seen Rice has been in my fantasies. He straightens and heads towards me. My jaw drops and I look at him questioningly.

He stops in front of me, leans down and whispers in my ear sending shivers down my body, "Fate's a fickle little thing, isn't she?" I feel his hands place something in mine. Then he straightens and takes his hand and gently pushes my jaw closed. "See ya on Thursday, cupcake."

He leaves me standing there and is almost out of the door

when I hear him yell, "Oh and sweets?" I turn around and walk out of the kitchen towards him and he nods his head towards the door Calder just left and adds, "I'm always up for a good fight. But I should probably warn you, I don't fight fair." Then he gives me a cocky little grin and a wink and walks out the door.

I glance down at what's in my hand and see the necklace my mom gave me. The one I thought I had lost forever. Kelly comes over and bumps me with her hip, "Girl, this is going to be fun."

ACKNOWLEDGEMENTS

I have to start off by thanking all of my family and friends. The support and enthusiasm you have all shown me over the last year has been beyond anything I could have dreamed. Your questions and genuine interest in my writing have blown me away.

To my boys: Thank you. Thank you for being willing to share me with my computer. Thank you for supporting me through this crazy ride. I love our perfectly crazy life. I love you more than any words can comprehend.

To my parents: Thank you for always supporting my dreams unconditionally. You two have been some of my biggest and loudest cheerleaders and for that I will always be grateful. Thank you for letting me overtake your house during deadlines

To my in-laws: Thank you for taking me in and treating me as your own. You guys are amazing examples of how in-laws should be. Thank you for all of your help and understanding during this crazy time. Thank you for raising an amazing and considerate man.

Jenn and Christie, I love you. You guys mean the world to me. The crazy times we have are some of my fondest memories. I look up to you two and hope to be as amazing of a wife, mother, sister, and friend as you guys are.

To my friends that are too numerous to name, thank you. I'm humbled by the sheer force of your love and support of me. The enthusiasm and excitement you guys have shown for this book has overwhelmed me. I love each and every one of you.

Brenna, you have been there every step of the way during this writing process. Thank you doesn't seem like enough to show how much your opinion and feedback has meant to me. You were always there talking me down from the ledge.

Felicia, this is probably going to get long. How can I even find words to tell you how much your friendship and guidance has meant to me? You have held my hand and given me the right pushes during this adventure. Your friendship is something I am going to cherish for the rest of my life. Love you, girlie!

Trish, I love knowing that I can ask you anything and you are always willing to help me out. I love you hard woman.

I'm so grateful for all the amazing people who have helped me on this journey. Sara Tharen, you are the best editor ever, seriously. Ashlee and Megan thank you so much for helping capture the perfect images for my cover. You two took what I was wanting and made it into something better than I could have imagined. Karen at Pampered Piglets, thank you for letting us use your land and pig for the cover shoot. Ginny and Raquel your feedback was monumental in helping get this book to where it is. So thank you! Jones I love you, all day every day. S. Moose you are and always will be one of my favorite people. You are so kind and caring. Rosie you are amazing. Everyday I'm grateful for our friendship. Jay and Jenn you girls crack me up, thanks for our friendship! Crystal, Brittainy, Alexis, Amber, Cori, Samantha, Silla, and Lisa thanks for being so willing to help out a noob like me. Between promoting, reading, and offering advice you all have been extremely kind. All of the blogs on my tour that have been so kind and supportive: The Got Books?, Got Books?, The Book Disciple, Those Naughty Girls Book Club, Jennifer Harper, Author Stalkers, Fictional Rendezvous Book Blog, One More Chapter, Fallen for Books, Adrienne Whitson, Renee Entress's Blog, Between the Lines, In The Pages of a Good Book, Book Crazy Friends, Angela's Book Desserts, Best Book Boyfriends, Whirlwindbooks, Bare Naked Words, Foxylutely Books!, MrsLeifs's Two Fangs About It, girlygirlbookreviews, and Beneath The Covers, thank you! There are about a million more of you that would take up to much space so just know that I am grateful for you and appreciate everything you have done for me.

ABOUT THE AUTHOR

L.J. Voss lives in beautiful Salt Lake City, UT with her husband, son, and dog. When she isn't writing, she can be found be reading or spending time with her family and friends. She loves the outdoors, listening to music, being crafty, and anything related to Nutella.

Made in the USA
Charleston, SC
11 July 2015